JO BARNES

Jo writes characters we can relate to, and some we won't want to! And she never just sticks to humans. There are elves, gods, foxes and dragons.

This is the third of Jo's books to be published and is the sequel to Wulf and the Power of Thorn. Jo loved both fantasy and the Anglo-Saxons and combined the two in her Wulf novels. She intended to write only one story about Wulf and his friends, but found she couldn't let her characters go.

Her first book was *Odd Fox Out*, a thrilling adventure about a fox who – rather inconveniently for him – decides he can't go on eating meat.

All of Jo's books are published by SilverWood Books and are available from booksellers and online.

ALSO BY JO BARNES

Odd Fox Out
Wulf and the Power of Thorn

WULF AND THE RUNES OF WODEN

JO BARNES

SilverWood

Published in 2026 by SilverWood Books
SilverWood Books Ltd
14 Small Street, Bristol, BS1 1DE, United Kingdom
www.silverwoodbooks.co.uk

Illustrations by Reena Patel

ISBN 978-1-80042-313-8 (paperback)

British Library Cataloguing in Publication Data
A CIP catalogue record for this book is available from the British Library

Page design and typesetting by SilverWood Books

For Angela, Derek, Penny and Vivien

WULF AND THE RUNES OF WODEN

CHAPTER ONE

Oz was so, so heavy. My breath was coming in painful rasps now. We had to get away, had to get back to the camp! His head was lolling on my shoulder and his arms were round my neck, but I couldn't stop his feet dragging along behind, catching on every tree root and bush. He was a dead weight, blood from his wound seeping warm and sticky through my leggings. He was so, so heavy.

Voices, a few yards away. I tensed. No! We'd left the Normans behind, hadn't we…? Thank God – English voices! It was Ranulf and Chad, veterans of more battles than me and Oz had had hot dinners. They crashed through the trees and stopped dead when they saw us.

"Give us a hand," I gasped. "Can one of you take his legs?"

"Here, give him to me," said big Chad. "I'll take him the rest of the way. Looks like you need to stop and take a breather."

"No time," I panted.

"Nah, it's all right," said Ranulf. "I reckon we've left them behind. We're safe for a bit."

But we weren't.

An arrow whizzed past Chad's head, almost nicking his helmet. I ducked, but Ranulf dived into the bushes towards the archer. Chad dumped Oz on the ground and ran after him. There was a cry and someone gabbling in that language that I hated so much, then a Norman soldier staggered towards me. But I didn't flinch. The soldier's arms were twisted behind his back and a knife was at his throat.

"I said, are there any more of you out there?" grunted Chad, who was holding the knife.

The soldier babbled something else, wild-eyed with terror.

"It'd help if we learned their lingo," said Ranulf. "Or they learned ours."

"If you can't talk English, shut up!" said Chad to the man, giving his arms a twist. "Go and have a look, Ran."

While Ranulf was gone I cradled Oz's head in my lap, but I didn't look at him. I couldn't take my eyes off the soldier's face. He'd lost his helmet and he didn't have a chain-mail hood. He had fair hair, like Oz. I hated the Normans, hated them for what they'd done to us, to our country, and hated them even more now for what they'd done to Oz. And yet…this soldier was only a few years older than me. His face was almost as white as Oz's and his eyes darted from side to side looking for a way to escape, but despairingly, knowing there wasn't one. What had driven him here to a foreign country? Had he been forced to come or had he chosen it, thinking it'd be an adventure? I knew Chad well. As loyal a friend as you could get but pitiless to his enemies, and I knew that this soldier's adventure was about to end.

Ranulf wasn't gone long.

"Nah, I told you they'd given up. This one must have got lost."

"Pity for him," grunted Chad. "Now why did you attack us if you were all on your little ownsome? You've got guts, but it ain't gonna do you any good now."

The man started mumbling something almost under his breath, but I caught a few words that I recognized.

"*Pater noster qui es in coelis…*"

He got no further for Chad slit his throat. I watched the crimson spurt as the soldier slumped to the ground. I felt numb. I was so tired. The first time I saw that happen I vomited, but not now. In the two years that me and Oz had been with the resistance I'd built a wall inside myself, cutting off my feelings. You had to or you'd go mad. This was dangerous, what I'd just been doing, thinking about the soldier as a person, wondering why he'd come. I mustn't do it again.

Chad kicked the body away and bent to pick Oz up.

"He doesn't look good," said Ranulf. "We'd better get a move on or *he'll* be a goner too."

Nobody spoke as we jogged back to camp. I tried not to think, which shouldn't be hard when you were this tired, but I couldn't quite manage it. This wasn't just any comrade Chad was carrying. This was Oz, my best friend, the brother I'd never had. I couldn't remember a time without Oz. We'd always been together, in the village, working in the fields, training at archery and swordplay and then fighting side by side in the battle. That battle that King Harold had almost won. And now for two years we'd been fighting in the resistance, sometimes winning, more often beating a retreat. I couldn't imagine a life without Oz.

But who was going to look after him when we got back? Alfwin did quite well on the whole, but this was bad. Oz had lost a lot of blood.

There was a moan and he shifted in Chad's arms. Thank God! Any sign of life was welcome. I clutched at straws as I refused to believe he could die.

It was dark by the time we got back to camp. Smells of roasting meat wafted from the fire but we ignored those and went straight to Alfwin's hut. He was outside stirring some herbal mixture over a fire.

"Oh, no," he sighed, "who have we got here?'

He looked worriedly at Oz and told Chad to carry him into the hut. But when he saw me his expression changed.

"I've got a surprise for you, lad," he said. "In there."

Puzzled, I followed Chad inside. In the light of a single lamp, a woman was bathing the shoulder wound of a man I hardly knew. He hadn't been with us long and I couldn't even think of his name. But I wasn't bothered about that because the woman turned round and looked at me. Her hair hung down in thick brown plaits. She nodded and her strong familiar face slowly broke into a smile.

I stood stock still with a mixture of amazement and delight.

"Mum!" I whispered.

CHAPTER TWO

"But how…" I stopped myself. "Tell me later, Mum. It's Oz!"

She looked at the figure in Chad's arms and she leapt up. Turning to the man whose shoulder she'd been bathing she said, "Alfwin will dress your wound now. It will soon heal."

Then Alfwin appeared and took over, as if he was the assistant and my mum was running the show. Typical. But that was exactly what I wanted. If anyone could save Oz, she could.

Chad laid Oz carefully on a straw pallet, raised his eyebrows at my mum, who ignored him, nodded at me and left. I stared at the front of his leather jerkin, stained with Oz's blood like the back of my leggings.

"Get my things, Wulf," said Mum, pointing at a battered leather shoulderbag in the corner of the hut.

I brought it to her and opened it, while she carefully cut away the cloth around the wound using Alfwin's knife. There was a deep gash in the top of Oz's thigh which was still bleeding heavily.

Alfwin looked across and frowned. "No vital organs there, Ertha, but that won't help if he doesn't stop bleeding."

Mum ignored *him* as well and rummaged in her bag, pulling out various packages of clean sacking. Sniffing them, she unwrapped one and pressed some dried leaves on to Oz's wound.

"Pity they're not fresh," she said to me, pushing down on the leaves. "Get me some water, and make sure it's clean."

I grabbed a wooden bowl from Alfwin's store and ran to the stream near the hut. When I got back, Alfwin had finished seeing to the young warrior and was watching Mum.

"You'll be needing a strip of leather and a stick," he offered.

Once again she ignored him and told Wulf to pour some of the water on to the leaves. Then she pressed down even harder.

"For a ligature," Alfwin went on.

I looked at him in horror, then at my mum.

"You're not going to cut his leg off, are you?"

I'd seen this done and even helped Alfwin twist the stick to tighten the leather strip. Even when it wasn't meant for an amputation but only to stop heavy bleeding like Oz's, the result was often a one-legged patient, sometimes alive, sometimes dead.

Mum rolled her eyes. "Find me the marigold, and I'll need some lavender, too."

I went rapidly through the packages, sniffing, as my mum had done, to find the right ones. The leaves were now sodden with Oz's blood and I handed her new ones.

"That's comfrey leaves, right?" I said.

"Good," she nodded.

"I can see where you get your know-how," said Alfwin. "He's been a good help to me."

Mum turned and stared at him. "Haven't you got something to do outside?" she said. And Alfwin suddenly found that, yes, he did actually have something to do outside.

When he'd ducked through the low doorway, I whispered, "He's all right really, and he does his best. I wouldn't push your luck."

Mum raised her eyebrows. "Tell me how this happened."

"Oz saved my life," I said simply, "so you've *got* to save his." All the while I was talking, Mum pressed the moistened herbs into the wound, but she listened intently.

"You remember Oz told you, when we came home just before we joined the resistance, how I sort of saved him. I just shoved him out of the way of this spear and it caught my jerkin, but I wasn't hurt. It wasn't anything big. I did it without thinking. Anyone would have. But he always felt he owed me one.

"And then today we were ambushed. This Norman came charging and chucked his spear and Oz threw himself at me and tried to shove me out the way and it caught his leg."

I stopped and shook my head.

"I was just lucky that time in the battle, and he wasn't".

Mum stopped pressing on the wound.

"What is luck?" she said. "I see you are still wearing Thorn."

I fished my rune-stone out of the front of my tunic. It looked like a worn old pebble with a shape faintly etched on the front. That shape was the rune Thorn, part of the ancient alphabet we had before the church came and gave us a new one. A hole had been drilled in the stone and a leather thong threaded through. I'd worn it round my neck ever since Mum gave it to me to keep me safe in the first battle against the Normans.

"There is your luck," she said. "Now help me bind this wound. It has stopped bleeding a little. We need clean comfrey leaves, and more marigold and lavender. Some strips of cloth, too."

"Oh, Alfwin's got plenty of those," I said, fetching a pile from a wooden chest. "He's quite a good healer. Not like you, of course."

"Hm," she muttered, setting to work. "Perhaps I should be a little nicer to him."

"Perhaps you should," I said.

"How long was Oz conscious before he blacked out?" she asked.

"Yeah, it was strange," I said, holding the bandaging firmly as she laid the different herbs between the layers. "He didn't look so bad at first. I mean he yelled when I pulled the spear out."

"What have I told you?" she snapped.

"Look, I know it's dangerous but it hadn't gone in that deep, and how was I supposed to get him away from there with a dirty great spear sticking out of his leg? I ripped off some of my tunic and stuffed it in the wound!"

"All right, all right," she nodded.

"And then he was moaning and groaning," I went on, "and I was trying to help him along while the others fought off the Normans. And then all of a sudden he collapsed on me. It was really quick."

I stopped, reliving what had happened.

"And…?" prompted Mum.

"Well, then he suddenly went dead white and his lips went blue and I just had to put his arms round my neck and drag him along. I mean, I know he was bleeding a lot, but I've seen other people with that sort of wound and they usually stay conscious for a long time."

"We need to move him somewhere private," said Mum, as she tied the strip of cloth. "Is there another hut?"

I jumped up and found Alfwin, who'd gone back to stirring his herbs.

"I'm sorry about my mum," I said awkwardly. "She was worried about Oz.

"She isn't usually like that," I lied.

Alfwin shook his head, then smiled at me. "It isn't your fault, boy. We can't help our families, but she obviously knows what she's doing."

"Oh yeah!" I agreed enthusiastically. "She does! And the thing is, she needs to move Oz to another hut where she can keep him really quiet."

"And use some of her unchristian magic on him, no doubt," said Alfwin.

I felt my face grow hot. I didn't know what to say.

"Don't worry, I've seen her sort before," Alfwin went on. "You can always tell. But as far as I'm concerned all healing must come from God, even if it comes in a roundabout way. We'll move Oz over there," pointing to a small hut on the very edge of the settlement.

I thanked him fervently and made up my mind to do the old man a favour as soon as I could. I was surprised though when my mum came outside and nodded her head at Alfwin.

"I have good hearing," she said. "I thank you and wish all were as open-minded as you."

It was dark in the new hut and the wavering flame of the tallow candle didn't reach the shadows around the walls. Oz's face looked a ghastly white in the small circle of light around the pallet. I started to lose hope.

"I need my runes," said Mum, as I knew she would.

I handed her the leather pouch but she shook her head.

"Empty them on to the ground," she said.

I opened the pouch and tipped them out, then turned to go. But something stopped me. Always at this point I'd left my mum, not wanting to see her runework, refusing to know anything about her magic. Now I stood, undecided. Why didn't I just go?

"I need Haegl to freeze the bleeding, Rad for his leg and Thorn to strengthen his heart."

I looked down and realized with a shock that I knew exactly which runes she was talking about. *But how…? How?* When she'd tried to teach me I'd told her I wasn't interested. More than that, I'd recoiled from them – I had no idea why – and she'd accepted that. I bent and scooped up the three runes, dropping them into her upturned palm.

"Wouldn't Wynn be helpful?" I heard my own voice saying, and picked up a fourth rune. *What?*

"Wynn is always helpful," Mum smiled and our eyes met. "It is your wyrd, Wulfstan, your destiny. You have always fought it, but it is your wyrd."

She turned to Oz and stroked his forehead with one hand while she gazed at the four runes in the palm of the other. Slowly she rocked back and forth chanting under her breath, while I stared numbly at the other runes on the ground. *Feoh, Ur, Ger…*I knew the names of all of them. *How was this possible?*

Suddenly she stopped chanting and her head jerked up.

"His spirit has been stolen!" she gasped. "I see it clearly now. Something was waiting to attack his spirit, waiting for the right moment, and the wound gave it a way in."

"Something?" I whispered. "What sort of something?"

She turned to me and for the first time I could remember I saw fear in her eyes.

"Something evil. And it is waiting for you too, my son."

CHAPTER THREE

I stood stock still. I felt as if all life and movement had drained away, leaving me like a lump of stone. I didn't doubt my mum, didn't wonder how she knew this. There was only one thing to ask. "What are we going to do?" I whispered.

Mum just sat there looking shaken. Then gradually she started to act a bit more like herself. She leaned across and took my hand. It was such an unusual thing for her to do that it shocked me out of my trance. I crumpled to my knees, clutching her hand. Then I looked at Oz's white face and that was the final jolt I needed.

"Never mind me!" I said. "It hasn't attacked *me* yet. But can you go on one of your spirit journeys and find Oz's soul – before it's too late? I'll keep everyone else away."

"Of course," she smiled. "Of course that's what I'm going to do. Meanwhile, don't get wounded or do anything to give this being a way to hurt you."

"You'll need some food," I said. Then, "Oh no, you don't, do you?"

Mum shook her head. "I've eaten since I arrived. You cannot journey on a full stomach. Some clean water though. And no-one must come near. I need absolute quiet."

I knew that. Knew that once her spirit was travelling it must not be disturbed. A wrong move could mean death for both her and Oz, as the link between soul and body was cut. In the old days, she'd told me many times, people knew this and they'd never disturb a healer on a spirit journey. But now the old knowledge was being lost, driven underground.

I saw that she had what she needed and sat down outside the doorway, leaning against the wall of the hut. It was deep night and most people had already settled themselves to sleep. The fires were low and the old moon was only a thin crescent but the sky was full of stars. I gazed up at them and gradually drifted into a trance. It seemed to me that a dark blue cloak had been thrown across to hide a blazing light up there in the heavens, and then someone had flown along piercing the cloak with a spear to let little points of light gleam through. I fixed my eyes on the seven bright stars of the Wagon, and imagined that I was up there among them, far away from the struggle that life had become.

A burst of laughter jolted me back to reality. Jumping up I went to find out who it was. Two young soldiers were leaning against the other side of the hut. I just hoped they hadn't disturbed Mum. They were meant to be on patrol but they'd stopped for a chat. Thank God, one of them was Hildred. He was from Lord Aelfric's estate like me and Oz.

"Hey, can you two be quiet," I whispered. "Oz is in there, practically at death's door, and he needs complete quiet. My mum's with him."

"Oh, sorry," said the other one. "We're supposed to be on patrol anyway. Guthlac'll have our guts for garters if he knows we're not keeping our eyes open."

"Right, you carry on," said Hildred. "I'll follow in a bit."

Hildred turned to me as his friend walked off.

"I was amazed to see your mum here today," he said. "Must be a couple of years since I last saw her."

"You and me both," I said. "You can't have been as surprised as I was. But you *did* know about Oz?"

"Yeah, bad is it?"

"Very," said Wulf. "That's why it's so important they're not disturbed."

Hildred nodded. "Ertha doing one of her special things, is she?"

I nodded back, relieved that I didn't have to explain more. Hildred's family had called on Mum a few times, despite the disapproval of the church.

"Don't worry, I'll keep things quiet…Sorry about Oz," he finished awkwardly, and went on patrolling.

I settled myself back outside the door and once again my eyes began to close. But why shouldn't I sleep? I was exhausted after everything – the fight, Oz getting wounded, struggling back to camp with him. And then all that stuff about the runes. How did I know what they were called? Some of Mum's knowledge must have seeped through, despite my best efforts not to learn it. And what *was* this thing that had captured Oz's spirit and was supposed to be after mine? I didn't know what I could do about that, but I didn't think staying awake would help. Why shouldn't I sleep? We were in camp, there were guards, and I was *so* tired.

I was woken by a hand roughly shaking my shoulder.

"Wake up, Wulfstan, for God's sake!"

Blearily I looked up into the face of Guthlac, the camp commander. It was bright daylight. Dawn had come and gone and the camp seemed to be full of people rushing around, scrambling over each other. So much for keeping things quiet for Oz and Mum.

"We've got to get moving," said Guthlac. "Word's come that we're all meeting up with Lord Edric at Shrewsbury and then we're headed for Wales."

"But..." I stuttered.

"Apparently there's a couple of Welsh princes willing to join forces with our lot," Guthlac continued, ignoring me. "Edric's hoping for a big push on the Normans quite soon."

"Yes, but..."

"Pretty good, eh? I've been waiting for this!" Guthlac clenched his fist. "We'll show 'em!"

"But Oz!" I finally managed to get out.

"Yes, I heard. Sorry about that, but we'll find a cart to carry him."

"No, you don't understand!" I said. "My mother's in there with him and she says he mustn't be moved!"

I didn't say that she mustn't be moved either, or they'd likely both end up dead.

"Yes, Alfwin said she's some sort of healer," said Guthlac. "Well, she can travel on the cart with him, can't she?"

"No, you don't understand!" I said again. But how could I *make* Guthlac understand? He wasn't like Hildred, who knew Mum, or even like Alfwin, who seemed to have some clue about her type of healing.

Guthlac stepped back and didn't look quite so friendly.

"These are orders, boy. You're a soldier, remember?" and he strode away.

I groaned. But…supposing Mum had already succeeded. There was a slight chance that she might have got Oz's spirit back and then they'd both be able to travel. Softly I lifted the latch of the hut and peered inside.

Oz was lying on the pallet like a corpse and Mum was crouched beside him, motionless, eyes shut. Very softly, I cleared my throat. Neither of them budged. I closed the door again and went running after Guthlac, who was shouting orders right and left. I grabbed his arm and Guthlac spun round, frowning.

"We can't come," I said before I lost my nerve.

"What do you mean, you can't come?"

"I'm sorry to disobey orders, I wouldn't if there was any other way, but we've got to stay here."

"*We?*" growled Guthlac.

"Oz and my mum," I said in a rush, "and I've got to stay to keep a look-out for them because he could die if he's moved and we'll come straight on as soon as he's well enough, leave us a cart or something and we'll follow on straight away." I paused for breath, shrivelling under Guthlac's glare.

There was a silence, finally broken by a deep sigh.

"I'll tell you something, son," said Guthlac, shaking his head. "You'll have to be a mighty good look-out, because the other reason we're moving is the Normans are coming this way. They'll probably be here in a few days. There's not enough of us here, so even if we weren't going to join up with Lord Edric and these Welsh princes, we'd have to decamp anyway."

"We'll follow on, I promise," I said weakly.

Guthlac nodded. "You've been a good fighter, and so has Oz. I hope you *will* follow on and not fetch up on the end of a Norman spear."

He turned and strode away.

I walked slowly back to the hut and peeped inside. No change there. Then all I could do was sit and listen numbly to the shouts and clatter, as the camp was taken to bits and all the people I'd come to know and trust prepared to go and leave me to face the Normans on my own.

The Normans and this…*thing*, whatever it was. This thing that had stolen Oz's soul.

CHAPTER FOUR

Guthlac left us some food and our own weapons, but in the end the carts were all needed.

"I'm sorry about this, son, but it's your decision," he said bluntly. "We can make room for him on a wagon along with all the other gear, but we can't leave a whole cart here just for Oz."

I looked on miserably as pots and pans and weapons were loaded on to the last wagon.

"So you understand," Guthlac went on. "It's on your head. Either we bring him now, which to me seems the obvious thing to do, or you'll all have to follow us on foot."

I shook my head. "Just go," I said. "We'll see you soon."

"I hope you're right," said Guthlac, but his expression said it was the last we'd be seeing of each other.

While everyone was calling out goodbye, Alfwin ran up with a leather bag.

"Take this," he panted. "I'm going to need most of my supplies, but I can spare a few bits if your mother runs out."

"Oh, thank you, Alfwin, thank you." I clasped the old man's hands. "You understand, don't you? You do understand that I'm not being awkward? I'd give anything to be coming with you, but we just can't."

Alfwin nodded. "I don't know exactly what your mother's doing, but I've known this kind of thing before. I've seen it work. It's just bad luck that we have to move on now."

"Come along, gaffer!" called a rough voice. "Get in the cart with your stuff or we'll leave you behind as well!"

Alfwin threw his arms round me. "God be with you," he said. Then he turned and climbed on to the last of the wagons, trundling along behind the last of the foot soldiers.

I was alone.

I walked slowly back to the hut, quietly lifted the latch and peered in. Mum and Oz might as well have been statues. They didn't seem to have moved an inch since I'd last looked. I sighed. What was I going to do with myself?

I'd go mad just waiting around. *Do something!* No need to go hunting yet – there was enough bread and cold meat for at least a day. I looked around at all the deserted huts. That's it. I'd make a thorough search of the village in case something useful had been left behind.

It had been a small but fairly well off little place until the Normans came. Now parts of it were burnt down and the villagers that were left alive had run away, but there were enough buildings left for Lord Edric's troops to use when they kicked the Normans out again.

Starting at the nearest hut I worked my way through the whole lot but there wasn't much left. Then in one dark corner I spied something white, a piece of bone which looked as if it had been sharpened. Some kind of weapon? I bent down and pulled it out. It had leather thongs attached and I smiled suddenly. A skate! It was small enough for a child's foot and as I stood holding it, tears welled up in my eyes. What had happened to this child when the Normans attacked?

It felt like yesterday that me and Oz and the other kids in the village had cheered when the river froze over. We'd fastened our skates on to our boots and raced the whole length of the river till it reached the boundary of Lord Aelfric's estate. That was what kids did, what they were supposed to do. Children were supposed to enjoy themselves.

And then the Normans came. I blinked away the tears and gritted my teeth. I'd show 'em! We'd all show 'em! The English'd never give in!

A cry broke the quiet. I dropped the skate, hared over to the hut where I'd left Mum and Oz and skidded to a halt outside the door. Then I opened it very, very carefully.

Mum was leaning back gasping for breath but Oz still lay pale and unmoving on the pallet. Then he blinked. His head moved slightly as he seemed to be trying to take in his surroundings. At last he saw me standing in the doorway and his face slowly broke into a smile.

"You're back then," I whispered.

"Looks like it," murmured Oz. "And I don't owe you one any more."

"No, I reckon we're quits," I said before flinging myself, half laughing, half crying, on top of him.

Only to be yanked off by Mum's strong hand.

"And what about me?" she said. "Don't I get a welcome? And don't you think the patient needs a little more time to recover before you start a wrestling match?"

"Ow! Sorry!" I said, rubbing my shoulder. Then I grinned at my mum and hugged her as well. I wasn't alone any more.

"All right, all right, that's enough," grumbled Mum, pushing me off. "We need something – some broth, perhaps. Nothing too much at first."

"Straight away," I said.

I went outside and started feeding the embers of the fire with little sticks, encouraging it back to life. Then I set a clay pot of broth in the ashes, blessing the soldier's wife who'd left it for us and feeling better than I had since Oz was wounded. We'd be all right now. My mum could heal anybody! Oz'd soon be well enough to travel, and the camp had only moved earlier that day. It was a pity they hadn't woken up in time to leave with everyone else, but that was all right. We'd catch them up in no time. I could hear my mum and Oz talking. He sounded fine.

But when I finally took two wooden bowls of broth inside, I realized that Oz wouldn't be going anywhere until at least tomorrow. He still looked deathly pale and had a job to sit up.

"Cheers, mate," he nodded, then pulled a face. "Mm, leek and onion, my favourite."

I laughed.

"You don't happen to have a mutton chop hiding up your sleeve, do you?"

"Be quiet, Osric," said my mum. "You're not ready for that yet."

"The thing is, Mum, we do need to move as soon as Oz is ready."

"Yes, where is everyone? It sounds as if we're the only people here."

"We are," I said, and told them what had happened. "So how long will it be before Oz can move?"

"It will take as long as it takes," sighed Mum. "But he is young and strong. Maybe tomorrow, maybe the day after."

I thought about the approaching Normans and some of my good mood trickled away. Mum looked at me with those piercing blue eyes that could see right through you.

"You are worried about the Normans," she said, "but that is not the only enemy you have to escape." She paused. "I am surprised, Wulfstan, that you have not asked me where we have been, Osric and I."

"Well, I was going to," I said guiltily, "but I haven't exactly had a chance. Tell me now then."

"When we have finished our broth," said Mum. "And have some yourself. We can do without you fainting from hunger."

I went to fetch myself some broth, feeling like a small boy who's been ticked off, my good mood now almost completely gone. Mum might be a great healer, but she could be a very irritating person.

"So who is this enemy?" I asked, supping from my bowl.

"It is, or was, a person," she said, "now in the spirit world. Once a great magician, I think, but now weakened. He is trying to regain his power, but how he is going to do this I am not sure. And he has a strong desire for vengeance. It obsesses his spirit, it consumes him. And the strange thing is, Wulf, I believe you know him."

"What?" I said. "I don't know anyone like that."

"Yeah," Oz joined in. "She keeps telling me I know him as well and I can't do. But the funny thing is…it's all a blur, what happened, like a really weird nightmare…but the funny thing is…there was this sort of evil presence, and I felt as if I had met it, or him before. But I can't have, can I? I mean, you wouldn't exactly forget if you met someone like that."

"No, you wouldn't," I said thoughtfully. My mum was usually right, but not this time.

Despite his moans Oz seemed to be relishing the broth. A good sign, I thought. And it *was* tasty. She was one of those people, the woman who'd given it to me, who could take any old scraps, give them something extra and dish up a delicious meal. Or perhaps we were all just hungry. Anyway, I thanked her again inside my head.

Steam from the bowl curled up my nose as I stared down into the greeny brown gloop. It definitely tasted better than it looked. I breathed in the steam and began to drift into a sort of trance, like last night, looking at the stars. Suddenly I yelled and spilled hot broth all over myself.

Two eyes had been staring back at me. Two dark eyes under a white deer skull, antlers spread wide. The eyes of someone unknown and at the same time horribly familiar.

CHAPTER FIVE

"What has happened?" said Mum, gripping my arm.

"A pair of eyes looking at me – in the bowl!"

"You had better rinse that off your tunic and then tell us what you are talking about."

"No!" said Oz. "I wanna know *now!* What d'you mean? One of the onions was looking at you?"

I snorted with laughter before gasping, "It's not funny, Oz. There was a pair of eyes in the bottom of the bowl!"

"Yuk!" said Oz. "I thought this was all vegetables."

"Oh, be quiet, Osric!" said Mum. "This is serious!"

"Sorry," said Oz. "I only wanna know."

"I think you left your brains behind in the spirit world," snapped Mum. "Come with me, Wulf."

She pulled me outside and down to the stream, where between us we washed most of the broth off my clothes. And all the while she was going on at me.

"Was it only eyes or did you see the whole face? Did you recognize him? Did you see anything else? Were you in a normal state of mind or were you slipping into a trance? Has this sort of thing happened before?"

The shock of the cold water helped me come to my senses so by the time we went back inside I could explain what had happened a bit more clearly.

"I think I *was* slipping into some sort of a trance," I said, "just looking into the broth and breathing in the steam. And in answer to your question, yes, I *do* do that sometimes."

"But when did you begin to do this kind of thing?" Mum asked. "It didn't happen when you were at home with me."

"Never mind all that," said Oz impatiently. "I wanna know what..."

Mum gave him a stare that would freeze a candle into an icicle.

"I think it started after the battle, two years ago," I went on. "It's nothing much. I don't black out or anything."

"And what exactly did you see?" asked Mum.

"*Now* we're getting to it," said Oz.

"Like I told you, a pair of eyes, really dark, piercing eyes, and it was like they were boring right into me, reading my thoughts."

"Whoa, disembodied eyes!" said Oz.

"No, they were in a face, but I didn't have time to notice much about the face. But I *did* see his headdress. Unless that was his actual head, but I don't think so."

"And the headdress?" said Mum.

"It was a deer skull. It had these really big antlers." I paused. "But the weird thing is...I think I *did* sort of recognize him...but how?"

My mum got up and started pacing round the edges of the little hut. It didn't take many steps to walk round the whole thing and me and Oz watched her as she paced, frowning at the floor. Then she stopped and looked up, swinging her heavy plaits back over her shoulders.

"I felt something," she said. "Two years ago, round about the time of the battle, when our king was killed. I felt something strange. It was a disturbance in the air, in everything around, a sort of ripple. I almost fell over, but no-one else seemed to notice anything. That means nothing, of course. Most people go around with their eyes shut, their ears blocked up and all their senses muffled. I have often wondered what it was, but found no answer. Now I wonder if that had anything to do with what is happening to you two. It may not, of course."

Oz shook his head. "I haven't got a clue what you're talking about."

"Listen, Osric, you said there was some evil presence there which you recognized but did *not* recognize."

Oz nodded. "Yeah, it sounds mad, doesn't it?"

"I felt this being," said Mum, "and although he was unknown to me, I had the feeling that you had met him before. And now Wulf says that he knows but does *not* know the face under the mask." She sighed. "I think perhaps…maybe there is some connection between what I felt two years ago…and the fact that Wulf sometimes drifts into a trance, which he certainly did not do before…and also between both those things and what is happening now."

Mum folded her arms and looked at us.

"Or of course, I could be completely wrong," she smiled. "At any rate, we will all soon need some sleep."

I groaned. "Mum, that all made no sense at all. You might as well have been talking that language the Normans talk."

"Come," she said. "I will wash these bowls in the stream. Wulf, see to the fire. Then both of you relieve yourselves and settle down for the night. It is getting dark and we need all our strength."

Oz needed help at first to stagger outside the hut, but by the time we went back in he seemed to have found his feet a bit. We lay down in the gloom of the hut and *he* was soon softly snoring.

But I couldn't sleep. Every time I closed my eyes the face under the skull swam into view, the expression shifting, sometimes mocking, sometimes threatening. At last I must have dozed off.

Crack!

What was that? I was wide awake now. I sat up. *Rustle, rustle.* It was probably an animal. Still, best to make sure. Cautiously I crawled to the door and peeped out.

It was pitch black inside the hut but the night sky was once again full of stars. They shed enough light for my eyes to scan the area. Everything was still, then…*there* – a moving patch of shadow. Yes, probably a fox, but a big one. Then the crouching shape unfurled itself and grew taller. With growing horror I watched as the fox revealed itself to be…a Norman soldier. He stood and looked around, his helmet silhouetted against the sky. I was frozen, not a muscle moving, not even breathing, but my mind was silently yelling one single desperate cry. *Don't let him come over here!*

Then while I watched, another thought crept into my head. The man was sturdier than me but I was growing fast and was probably the same height. And I had the element of surprise. The soldier seemed to be on his own, probably doing some sort of scouting. The village was empty. He wouldn't be expecting an attack from behind. I didn't have any armour on but I had my sword. And the man was standing right by the hut where I'd found the skate. Some *other* soldier had been there, had done something to the child who owned the skate. I couldn't hurt that first soldier, but I could take revenge on this one! They were all as bad as each other, the Normans. I felt for my sword in the dark hut and crouched by the door.

"*Ici*", called the soldier. "*Je suis ici!*" and another man walked into view.

They stood talking and I found that I was shaking and running with sweat. What a fool I was! I'd nearly got myself killed! I heard Guthlac's voice in my head. *Don't do anything rash. A canny soldier lives to fight another day.*

The two men walked off and I heard horses softly whinnying and clopping away into the night. My hand was sweating so much that I had to wipe the hilt of my sword dry. So the Normans were nearer than we'd thought. Much nearer.

I listened to Oz breathing heavily on the straw pallet. He wasn't well enough yet, but…

I gently shook my mum's shoulder.

"Wake up," I whispered. "We've got to go."

CHAPTER SIX

Very early the next morning, before the sun was up, we helped Oz on to his feet. Mum had put Alfwin's extra supplies of herbs and bandages into her own leather bag and I was carrying Alfwin's bag, now filled with the cold meat and bread we'd been left. I had Oz's sword and Mum took his bow and arrows. But the main thing we were carrying was Oz. It felt like it anyway, he was leaning on us so heavily. If only we had a cart. Or if only Mum and Oz had returned from the spirit world just a few hours earlier.

The little village had felt like home but it was silent now and looked dead in the cold, grey light before dawn. I'd heard those soldiers riding away, but how far had they gone? One thing was certain – we'd have to try and stay out of sight.

"This is the life," grinned Oz. "Off for a nice early morning stroll with everyone else carrying my gear."

"I suppose I have to get used to your eternal joking again," sighed Mum. "I thought you might have grown out of it by now."

"Well, what d'you want him to do?" I said. "Sit down and cry?"

"No, no. It is better to be like that. But I do not think he will feel much like laughing soon. Come on, we must get started."

We filled our water flasks at the stream and set off.

But it was hard going. Oz was limping and he still didn't have much strength. It was a sunny autumn day and we had to keep stopping so he could have a drink and a rest. I was tired too as we flopped down to eat our midday meal.

"I'm sure you're heavier now than you were this morning," I moaned.

My mum gazed ahead, chewing her bread and meat, and didn't seem to be aware of us. But when Oz reached toward the provisions bag she slapped his hand away without even looking.

"We've got to make it last," she said, still staring ahead.

"I'm just asking," said Oz, "but do we know exactly where we're going?"

"North west," said Mum, "towards Shrewsbury."

"There's miles and miles to go yet," I said, "and it'd be easier on a proper road, but we can't risk it."

"Come," said my mum, brushing herself down. "Every step is one step nearer."

The food and rest seemed to have had a good effect on Oz. He didn't lean on us so heavily and even tried a few steps on his own.

This looked like good fertile country but a lot of it was laid waste by fighting and crops being burnt. So when we passed an orchard with trees still bearing apples it seemed like an unexpected gift.

"It'd be a crime to let these go to waste," I said.

I climbed a few trees and threw fruit down to them till they'd filled their bags. Then we all sat down to enjoy a crisp, juicy apple apiece.

"How long d'you reckon before we get there?" I asked.

Mum shrugged.

"Well, at this rate," said Oz, "I reckon we'll be just in time for Christmas."

"Come on then," I sighed. "We'd better keep an eye out for somewhere to spend the night." I paused. "You're very quiet, Mum."

"Why talk if there is nothing to say?" she replied, and I looked at her. It was true, she never did talk much, but there was something about her silence that made me uneasy.

We plodded on as the shadows lengthened, until Oz spotted a hut in the distance. It looked like a cow byre and a deserted one at that, but you couldn't be too careful. I went ahead, keeping low as I got near the hut, and was relieved to find it as empty as it looked. I jogged back and me and mum helped Oz the final few hundred yards. He staggered inside and collapsed.

"Good," nodded Mum, as she looked around. There was straw to sleep on and a roof over our heads.

"Our second bit of luck," I said. "First the orchard, now this."

"Yeah, I'm feeling really lucky," groaned Oz, lying flat out on the hay.

"Let me look at your leg," ordered Mum.

She stripped off the dressing, cleaned the wound and applied some more herbs and a fresh bandage.

"It's doing well," she said. "No more bleeding. Now lie still while I speed up the healing a little."

Oz shut his eyes. "Heal away," he said. "I'm not going anywhere."

I studied my mum as she placed her hands over the wound, close but not quite touching it. I knew what Oz would be feeling – the warmth, the tingling, but now I wondered how it was for Mum. She had a look of intense, calm concentration on her face. I wondered if *I* could do that and just as the thought popped into my mind Mum spoke, without moving her hands or looking at me.

"Yes, my son, you could do this if you practised, if you really wanted to."

I was used to her reading my thoughts, but it was still a bit off-putting.

"And it could be useful," she went on. "I shall not always be with you."

Well, obviously not, I thought. And a good thing too, added a little voice in my head. Immediately I felt guilty and shut the voice up. I glanced at her, but she showed no sign of having overheard that particular thought. And why did the little voice say that? Perhaps because I'd started to feel like a man in the last two years and she often seemed to treat me like a small boy. Still, it *was* a comfort to have her here at the moment. Feeling confused but too tired to think about it, I drifted off to sleep.

The next morning Oz looked far more like himself. He could stand easily and walk quite a few steps without help, so we made much better progress. Then after our midday break we came across what I reckoned was our "third stroke of luck."

"Is that what I think it is?" I said, peering into a ditch.

An upturned cart was stuck in the mud at the bottom.

"Leave it," said Mum. "It is too small and probably broken."

"It doesn't look broken," I said. "It just looks stuck. And if it isn't broken it'll be brilliant. Oz can have a ride sometimes and we can shove all our gear on it the rest of the time."

I scrambled down, dug around, getting filthy in the process, and heaved. The cart came free with a sucking sound.

"Here you are," I said. "Take a handle each. You pull and I'll push."

Oz grabbed one handle but when Mum touched hers she pulled her hand away as if she'd been stung.

"Got a splinter?" asked Oz.

"It is nothing," she said, and once again grasped her side of the cart.

I looked at her face and saw that she was lying. It wasn't "nothing", but I knew better than to ask.

Once the little wagon was on level ground we had a good look.

"Why would anyone leave a cart down there if it's not broken?" I wondered.

"Well, thicko," said Oz. "How about you're trying to escape the Normans, your cart falls down a ditch and you think to yourself, now shall I rescue my cart and get a Norman arrow in my back or shall I just leave it?"

"S'pose so," I said. "Wanna ride?"

Oz grinned, climbed in and made himself comfortable.

"You can carry these yourself now," I said, dumping Oz's sword and bow in beside him. "*And* these," I added, throwing the two bags in as well. "All set, Mum?"

She didn't say anything but I could see her flinch as she took hold of the cart handle. I decided to ignore it. We were following a rough dirt track and the ground here was level. Even so, I realized that pulling a laden cart was not as easy as I'd thought. I wasn't sure what we'd do when the ground began to climb.

Suddenly Mum stopped.

"Listen!" she commanded.

We listened. Silence, apart from the occasional burst of birdsong. Then…a slight rumbling in the distance. She dropped to the ground and put her ear to the earth.

"Horses," she said. "Many horses, coming from behind us."

"So it can't be *our* troops!" I said.

Me and Oz looked wildly around, but Mum had already spotted a line of trees in the distance.

"We must hope that is a wood," she muttered, as we pulled with all our might.

"I'm getting out," said Oz. "We can all move quicker if the cart's lighter."

"Shall we just leave it?" I panted.

"Nah," said Oz. "I'll push. I'm a lot better. It's too useful to leave."

I looked to Mum for a decision but she stared grimly ahead.

The land was criss-crossed with ditches like the one where we'd found the cart, and they weren't always easy to spot till you were on top of them. Me and Mum strained to pull the cart and Oz pushed from behind, head down, trusting us to guide it.

Suddenly a ditch appeared at our feet. That was how it seemed. One minute it wasn't there and then it was, giving us no time to stop. I lost my balance, teetered on the edge and managed to haul myself upright by hanging on to the arm of the cart. It twisted sidewise towards my mum and in the split second it took for all this to happen Oz carried on pushing, quite unaware of what was going on. The wagon teetered, then toppled headlong into the ditch, with Mum underneath.

There was an agonised scream.

"Mum!" I cried.

I leapt down and heaved at the cart, while Oz scrambled down after me. Between us we managed to get it on its side and free her, but she didn't move. She lay grimacing in agony, as trapped as if the wagon was still crushing her. One leg was twisted beneath her and the other stuck out sideways in a position that should be impossible for a human leg. Worst of all, a piece of white bone was piercing the skin. I stared at it, as blood slowly began to seep out. Mum's face was as white as the bone.

"Give me my knife," she gasped.

"What for?" I said numbly, trying to think, my mind whirling round like a flock of starlings.

"Just give it to me," whispered Mum. "I can't reach it."

Her belt had twisted round so that the knife was underneath her. I bent down to ease it out of its sheath. *I didn't know what to do!* I didn't know what to do, and it was easier just to do what I was told.

"You are brave boys," breathed my mum, so softly that we both leaned nearer to hear her. "I am proud of you. Now you must escape, reach those trees and go on to join our men."

"But how can we leave you?" I asked, handing her the knife. Afterwards I wondered how I'd let myself give it to her. Was it sheer force of habit? She wasn't someone you disobeyed. And I had no idea what she was going to do with it.

"You must go or we will *all* be killed," she choked. "And that is useless, useless!"

"We'll manage," I said desperately. "You can go in the cart, Oz is stronger now, we'll manage," I babbled.

Mum smiled through her pain, but she shook her head.

"It is my wyrd, my son. And it is your wyrd to try and rid our land of these accursed invaders."

"No, I'm not gonna leave you!" I sobbed, my eyes pricking with tears.

Mum let out one long rasping breath.

"Just go. Just go," she whispered. "I knew that cart would be my doom, but I had to accept it. The three sisters have cut the thread of my life."

And we watched in dumb horror as she plunged the knife into her midriff.

CHAPTER SEVEN

Blood oozed from the wound and bubbled from her mouth with her last breath.

"No," I moaned. "No."

It was impossible. How could someone so strong be dead? How could I have thought last night, even for a moment, that I didn't want her around? We *needed* her. We *both* needed her. She'd saved Oz and now she was gone. I looked at Oz, but I couldn't see him clearly with my eyes all blurry. I wiped the tears and snot from my face with my sleeve. Oz crouched pale and motionless, staring down at Mum, who'd been almost as much a mother to him as she had to me.

Then he looked back at me and blinked.

"We've got to go," he said. "We've got to escape, or she might as well not have killed herself."

I nodded. "We can't leave her like this," I said, "and we've got no time."

"Cover her with the cart," said Oz. "We can come back later and bury her properly."

Mum was tall and the cart wasn't big enough to hide her body, so we gently laid her on her side and curled her up like a sleeping baby. I kissed the top of her head.

"The knife?" said Oz.

"Leave it!" I snapped.

Her hand had let go of the dagger in her death spasm, and I bent her fingers round it once again. I don't know why I did it. It just seemed the right thing to do. Then we lowered the cart over her, grabbed our weapons and bags, climbed out of the ditch and ran.

We sped towards the trees on the horizon, Oz with no sign of an injured leg. I glanced back. I couldn't see anything but I could hear more clearly now the sound of an approaching army. Had we left it too late? Should we just have left Mum as she lay? No! We had to do something to hide her. Even if that meant our deaths. I stopped thinking and concentrated on the line of trees, which still seemed a long way away.

We were both panting and Oz suddenly stumbled and cried out. I crouched down beside him.

"Is it your leg?"

Oz nodded, gritting his teeth. "It was okay just now, then it gave way. You go on."

"Don't be daft!" I snorted. "Look, I don't think we'll be seen if we crawl along the ground. Could you do that?"

Oz nodded. "But we'll never get there like that," he said.

"Yes we will. Come on, I'll take both the bags."

So we shuffled along, painfully slowly it seemed, until we reached the nearest trees of what turned out, thank God, to be a small forest.

Oz groaned and propped himself against a beech tree.

"Must have a drink," he gasped.

I took out the two leather flagons of water and a couple of apples and we sat in exhausted silence.

Finally I said, "We'd better get further into the wood," and helped Oz to stand up.

Our feet crunched on fallen leaves, though the trees weren't quite bare yet.

"Two years ago," said Oz, leaning on me, "it was just like this. Two years ago when we were running away from the Normans the first time."

I didn't say anything. Would it ever end? Fighting, gaining a bit of ground, retreating.

Finally, when the wood was at its most dense and even the birds seemed to have stopped singing, we collapsed once more. It was clear we wouldn't be going any further that day. Even if the light hadn't been growing dim we had no energy left to struggle on. So we made ourselves as comfortable as we could in a hollow between two roots of an enormous oak, and we shared out our rations.

"We've gotta leave something for tomorrow," I said. "The day after that can take care of itself."

We ate in silence.

Then, "We're lost," said Oz.

"I know," I said, "but I'm sure we can work out where we're going when we're feeling a bit better. But first I'm gonna try some of that healing on your leg."

Oz laughed. "You gonna turn into your mum?" he asked, and broke down.

"It's all right! It's all right," I said, tears streaming down my own face. I leaned over and hugged Oz and we sat and wept.

At last Oz pulled away and wiped his face.

"D'you remember that time we were mucking around and nearly set the cottage on fire?" he said. "God, wasn't she mad!"

"I know," I grinned. "We ran away and hid in the tithe barn, and she found us and walloped us both. It was stupid hiding really. I mean, we'd have had to come out at some point."

"Little kids *are* stupid, aren't they?" sniffed Oz.

I sighed. "You know...I was always glad when you were there," I said. "It was like having a brother. And the thing is, I know she was glad too."

"You reckon?" said Oz.

"Yeah, I'm sure of it," I said.

We sat for a while without talking and then Oz said, "She was a great story teller, your mum. She never said much the rest of the time, but boy could she tell a story. I used to like those ones about the old gods."

I laughed. "She used to say to me, 'There is no need to mention these tales to that priest!'"

I could feel myself start to choke up again, so I stopped. It was quite dark now and if I didn't talk Oz wouldn't be able to tell I was near tears.

"We should go to sleep," said Oz. "Back to back with both our cloaks over us."

"You're right," I said, and then roused myself. "No, let me try a bit of healing first."

"You serious?" said Oz. "You won't be able to see what you're doing."

"I don't need to *see*." I leaned across and felt for Oz's leg.

"Ow!" said Oz.

"Well, I've hit the right spot anyway," I said. "Just keep still."

I put my hands palms down a few inches above Oz's wound and shut my eyes. Then I jumped. I'd heard my mother's voice in my head!

"*Be still, Wulf,*" it whispered, "*and feel the life force flowing from your hands into the wound.*"

Waves of warmth pulsed through my hands and out towards Oz's leg, and I stayed quite still and let it flow through me. I could do it! I could heal. 'It isn't you doing it,' Mum always said. 'It's life itself using you as a channel.'

After a while my arms started to ache and I lowered my hands.

"Not bad," breathed Oz. "Not as good as your mum, but not bad. Who'd have thought it?"

"Now go to sleep," I grunted. The last thing I wanted to do was talk about it.

Oz rolled over and I settled myself with my back against his. The smell of leaf mould was strong in my nostrils as I lay, quietly turning everything over in my mind. I could tell by the even breathing that Oz was soon asleep but there were too many thoughts and memories drifting around my head. That probably hadn't been Mum's voice, I was probably just remembering what she'd told me about healing. But, still, it was very comforting. It made her feel closer. It made me feel less abandoned.

I reached my hand inside my shirt and pulled out the ancient runestone on the thong round my neck: the stone my mum had given me when I went to fight alongside King Harold. There'd been some story about it belonging to Woden, the king of the gods, though she'd obviously taken that with a big pinch of salt. "Believe that and you'll believe anything," she'd laughed. "Still," she went on, "wear it and it will keep you safe." She'd wanted me to be safe. She'd wanted to help me and I felt that, somehow, she still did. I held the rune-stone in front of my face, but it was too dark to see.

Suddenly a shaft of moonlight pierced the dark and shone on the stone. The shape of the rune danced in the moonbeam, shimmered in front of my eyes and then...I was in a different forest.

Instead of leaf mould I could smell the rich scent of pine needles. I was in a forest glade with giant pine trees all around. Stars shone brightly overhead but brighter still was a full moon. Was it the same moon that had woken up the rune-stone? A fire was crackling and dancing in the middle of the glade. I could feel its heat though I was some yards away. A tall, cloaked figure was sitting on a log by the fire, while two ravens strutted their jerky walk around the flames. The figure turned to me. The broad brim of his hat was pulled down over one eye, and the other eye looked at me in a way that was neither friendly nor unfriendly.

"Ah, you've come back," he said.

CHAPTER EIGHT

I stared at him.

"What?"

The figure in the clearing sighed. "I *said*, you've come back."

I blinked. What was going on?

"Back?" I said. "I've come *back*?"

"Dear me," tutted the man. "How long is this conversation going to go on?"

My mind raced back and forth, trying to remember. *Had* I been here before? There *was* something vaguely familiar about both the cloaked figure and the clearing. And the ravens! Who had two ravens? It couldn't be...could it? I gazed at the man with a creeping feeling of awe and wonder and he stared back at me, tilting his head slightly so that I could see his face more clearly under the brim of his hat.

He had one eye! The other socket was empty!

I gasped and fell to my knees. Then I bowed my head and waited.

"You know who I am," said Woden.

"Yes, Lord," I stuttered, "but honestly, I honestly don't really remember being here before."

A thought darted into my head. Perhaps Woden was mistaken? Perhaps he thought I was someone else? But no, gods didn't make that kind of mistake. Not this one anyway. Not the Allfather, the king of the gods.

One of the ravens flapped his wings and hopped on to Woden's shoulder. He cawed softly into the god's ear and Woden laughed.

"Thank you, Muninn," he said. "My friend is reminding me that those annoying elves enchanted you. They took away some of your memories, including that of our previous meeting."

Elves? What elves? What *was* he talking about?

I sat back on my haunches. The firelight played on Woden's face, on the shrivelled socket where his eye should be, the eye that he had given up in return for a deep draught from the well of wisdom. A breeze rustled the branches of the pine trees, the ravens murmured soft cawing sounds, the fire crackled and I surrendered myself to it all. I hadn't got a clue what was going on but it didn't matter. I was in the presence of the one who my mum had honoured above all others: Woden, master of the runes.

"Now what is the best way to return your memories to you, I wonder," said the god.

Munin hopped down from his master's shoulder and the other raven flapped up and settled himself down. He too cawed softly into Woden's ear, then sat back and cocked his head on one side.

"Ah, yes," nodded Woden. "Thank you, Huginn. I was thinking of that myself. Since we both agree, that must be the best course of action."

Huginn looked at me with what seemed suspiciously like smugness in his beady raven eyes. *Huginn*...Huginn was doing the thinking and Muninn seemed to be remembering things. Yeah, that was it. My mum had told me: Huginn meant *thought* and Muninn meant *memory*. Woden's two ravens who flew all over the world and reported back to him what was happening.

"A bindrune, I believe," Woden went on. "I used this on you before and it worked well. Different runes, of course."

I nodded. "All right," I muttered cautiously. Well, it was going to happen whatever I said, but I felt I had to say something.

"I shall use Perthro and Mannaz," said Woden.

The raven on the ground cawed loudly and Woden laughed again.

"Muninn has remembered that you prefer me to use their English names."

"I do?" I said. It was off-putting that they all seemed to know more about me than I knew about myself.

"So, if you like, I shall call them Peorth and Mann. Also Wunjo, I think, which you would call Wynn."

I thought that I wouldn't call any of them anything, since I'd never bothered to learn their names. Although...I *had* remembered them the other night, when I'd shaken Mum's runes out of their bag.

"Peorth is good at uncovering memories hidden deep within, but it could leave you feeling confused."

Hardly more confused than I was feeling now!

"Mann is the rune of humanity and of the intellect. It will help you to make sense of what you remember," Woden went on. "And Wynn, the rune of joy and harmony will, I believe, help you to bring past and present into harmony. Wynn is always good to use in a bindrune, don't you think?"

Woden smiled and raised an eyebrow. He's playing with me, I thought. He knows I don't know what he's talking about. *Or do I?* Because that's what I'd said to my mum. *Wouldn't Wynn be helpful?* And she'd said, *Wynn is always helpful.*

I stared at Woden. You know all this, I thought. You know everything I've said and done.

"But I have another way of helping you to remember," said Woden, "as well as the runes. Muninn – are you ready?"

I was still on my knees and the raven puffed himself up and strutted up and down in front of me. Woden bent to take a stick from the edge of the fire. He raised it in the air and pointed the glowing end at my forehead. I shrank back.

He drew three fiery rune shapes in the air and each remained, hovering where Woden had drawn them. He pulled the righthand one into the centre and then the lefthand one, so that all three runes mingled into one dazzling pattern, dancing before my eyes.

Muninn stopped marching back and forth and stood right in front of me, cocking his head first one way and then the other. His little black eyes bored into mine as he waited for his master's command.

There was silence, and I began to feel very afraid. Then two things happened at once. Woden flicked his wrist so that the bindrune shot into my forehead like a bolt of lightning. I cried out and fell backwards, but as I fell the raven opened his beak and gave one deafening caw. It blasted in my head like a thunderclap to go with the lightning, coming from all directions at once, surrounding me with a wall of noise.

Then the flash of the bindrune became the glint of spears waving in the sun and the caw became the noise of an army cheering and I was back in the battle against Duke William. But our King was alive! How could this be? The arrow had only grazed his eye! Reinforcements had marched in from Mercia! The cry went up, "God bless King Harold!" And the Normans were being driven back! They were routed! *But that wasn't what happened.* What was going on? It seemed so real, yet it wasn't what had really *happened.* Gradually, gradually it dawned on me that somehow this *was* what happened. Somehow, in a way that made no sense to me, I knew that this wonderful thing, the English victory over the Normans, really did happen. I was filled to the brim with joy and wonder.

And the next second I was at the victory feast, laughing and getting drunk with Oz and after that the pictures sped through my mind, each one giving me just enough time to remember what was going on. Me and Oz, kidnapped, escaping, but not just the two of us. Bronwen was with us, the dark-haired Welsh girl I'd liked so much. And then a man was with us, a foreign-looking man dressed all in black. Abdul, he was called. Then some little people, only about three foot high. Yes, *elves*!

More pictures flashed by, and a warrior magician was about to kill us all but I took my rune-stone and said...and said..."By the power of Thorn I command you to stop!"

A jolt of energy surged through me, now, in the clearing with Woden, and I clutched my rune-stone, the ancient stone that my mum had given me, that had once belonged to Woden, and I felt its great power. I'd used those words and the warrior had frozen.

Then the pictures raced even more quickly, a jumble of people, places and monsters.

Me and Oz were captured by another magician, a powerful sorcerer. I shuddered as I remembered the sense of evil that had flowed from this man. Then Oz was in a dungeon and I'd been shown by one of the elves how to concentrate on my rune-stone and I'd suddenly found myself... *here*! Yes, here, in this clearing with the two ravens and the cloaked and hatted Woden. I *had* been here before!

And Woden had told me to do something, and I had to do it or the world could unravel in the time shift the sorcerer was planning. Then I was at a magic ceremony and there was the sorcerer, with a stag's skull on his head. There he was, the figure I'd seen in the bottom of the bowl! And then the sorcerer – what was his name? – *Gethin*, that was it! And as I said the name inside my head, Gethin turned and looked at me, *now*, in the present, his dark eyes boring into mine, an evil smile on his face. A shockwave convulsed me, here, in the clearing. He was looking for me. He was looking *at* me. I gasped, but the pictures drew me back into the story.

There was Gethin at the ceremony, slitting Oz's arm open, feeding the circle of runes with Oz's blood. Then Gethin worked his spell and I was whisked back years, centuries with him, to a time before the English came to these islands. Lightning split the sky, thunder shook the air and the ground beneath my feet juddered. The ground split open and I managed to do whatever Woden had told me and Gethin fell. He fell into the fiery chasm at his feet. And I thought the magician was dead. He *was* dead! But here he was, somehow, from the other side of death, still working evil.

Then I was whirled forward in time again, back to the battle. But what had happened? *What had happened?* Something had changed in the time shift. The Mercians didn't arrive. No reinforcements came. Harold went down when the arrow grazed his eye and the Normans fell on him! They hacked him to pieces. They killed the king. The battle was lost.

A deep despair grabbed hold of me and wrung every scrap of hope and joy out of my heart. We lost. We lost. Because of Gethin's time shift the battle had turned out differently. But Woden had charged *me* to make sure everything came out right. And it hadn't. So if I'd done something differently...if I'd managed, somehow, to have more control of things instead of being buffeted about by the winds of magic and time...if I'd *tried* harder...could we have won? Could that amazing victory I'd seen at the beginning really have been ours?

Slowly I raised my eyes and stared at Woden.

"It was my fault. It's my fault we lost. I wish I was dead."

CHAPTER NINE

Woden sighed a long, deep sigh.

"I think you have been infected by this new religion, this Christianity. All this guilt. *Mea culpa, I have sinned.* That's what they say, isn't it, in those churches? Now tell me, Wolfstone, in what way is it your fault that the English lost the battle?"

I swallowed. Tears pricked my eyes as I struggled to find the words.

"You told me…you told me I had to do something," I stuttered. "With the runes. I had to stop Gethin going back in time and I didn't. In that magic ceremony. I nearly did it, but not quite." I stopped, but not because I was trying to remember. All those memories were seared into my brain now, perhaps even more clearly than if I'd never forgotten them in the first place. I stopped because it was so painful. We'd won the battle, then time had changed and we'd lost. All the terrible things that had happened since the Normans arrived might never have been. Instead, we could have been basking in that glorious feeling of triumph, that feeling I'd had in the victory celebrations. Life could have been so sweet.

"And did you give up?" said Woden. "Did you think, oh well, that's that, I've failed?"

"No," I admitted. "I hung on. I went back in time with him. I killed him – sort of. I caused his death, anyway. But then we came back and I might as well not have bothered because everything had changed. He won, in a way. He was trying to stop the English coming here, all those hundreds of years ago, but if he couldn't do that, then the next best thing was to have us defeated by the Normans. Make us slaves in our own country."

"Ah, you might as well not have bothered," nodded Woden. "And do you remember what was happening to the world when this sorcerer rolled back time? Was it a peaceful, moonlit night when you travelled back with him?"

"No," I said. "There was a terrible storm and an earthquake…"

"Which would have got worse and worse," interrupted Woden, "until the whole of middle earth had disintegrated." He shook his head. "His pride, this sorcerer, to think that he could turn back time to right his own petty grievances." Woden clasped his hands together and gazed into the fire. "Where was I? Ah yes, and who was it who stopped the world from disintegrating?"

Silence. The fire crackled, a breeze rustled the pine tree branches, but I didn't say anything.

Then, at last, "Well, I suppose it was me," I whispered.

"Oh, surely not *you*," Woden pretended to be surprised. "Not the great failure, the one whose *fault* it is that the Normans won the battle? It surely could not have been you who *saved the world*?"

I looked at him, unsure what to say.

"And did you not know," Woden's voice was rising now, beginning to sound angry. "Did you not know that all great undertakings involve risk? Risk that things might not turn out for the very best? But that they might still be a great deal better than if the risks had not been taken?"

Muninn cawed loudly and I jumped.

"My friend Muninn is telling me," said Woden, "that he heard that wretched elf Pooka warn you that time is a tricky thing. He *told* you that no-one could be certain where things would end up, or that circumstances would be the same if time were played with."

Woden stood up and I shrank back. I felt tiny, insignificant. The god was very tall and his one eye burned fiercely as he glared at me.

"Now stop feeling sorry for yourself!" he shouted. "I have work for you to do and I need the hero who saved the world, not some snivelling wretch!"

Hero? Was Woden calling me a *hero*? Or was he playing with me?

"No, I am not playing with you!" snapped Woden. "We don't have time for all this. There's work to do."

I was torn between annoyance at having my thoughts read and amazement at what I'd just been told. I'd saved the world? I, Wulf, was like one of the heroes of old? I sat up straighter and started to feel that, yes, I *was* capable of doing great things. Suddenly, I remembered feeling like this once before, just after the battle when the king had been killed. I'd thought that was because I'd been pleased I'd saved Oz's life. Then over the last two years I'd been worn down by the non-stop fighting, the few victories, the constant retreats. I'd lost that good feeling inside myself. But, looking back, wasn't it strange that I'd felt so good when we'd just lost that great battle with the Normans? Was it really possible I'd felt like that because I'd stopped the world from falling to pieces?

"Wolfstone, listen to me! The sorcerer's body died but his spirit lives on. He has aligned himself with the forces of chaos, those who seek constantly to destroy the world. He is so full of hate for the English that he no longer cares what happens to anything else, even his beloved Wales, so long as the English are destroyed. And especially *you*!"

I tried to concentrate but it was hard to take it all in.

"He needs my rune-stones, the ones he had gathered into his castle. There are a few others, including yours, but most are still there. I need you to find them and return them to me."

"But what about rejoining our forces? Fighting the Normans?"

"Forget that! That war is lost!"

"What?" I felt as if my head was imploding. The one thing that had kept us going was the thought that we could get rid of the invader. And now Woden was telling us to give up.

"You're supposed to be the god of battle!" I said hotly. "How can you tell us to give up?"

Woden bowed his head and stood still and silent for a few moments. Then once again he sighed deeply.

"It is not easy for me to say that. England has been defeated but she will rise again...gradually. And then she will be truly great. But for now other things are more important. You are right, Wolfstone, I am a battle god. But tell me now, what else am I the god of?"

I thought. “You’re the god of the runes…and poetry, too…And you’re the god of magic.”

Woden nodded. “Well said. And to use my magic fully, to fight the forces of chaos, I need those rune-stones. I imbued them with powers which must, at all costs, be kept from our enemies.”

“But why can’t you just take them?” I asked. “Walk in middle earth in disguise, the way you used to?”

“You asked me something like that once before,” said Woden. “Alas, times have changed. My followers are few, so my power in middle earth has waned. It is easier for you, a child of middle earth, to complete this task. The sorcerer Gethin has the same problem. He cannot now walk in the world of the living, but must find someone to do his work for him.” He paused, then went on matter-of-factly, “And, of course, you’ll have to explain all this to Osric.”

“*What*? You’re joking!”

“I’ll send Muninn with you,” said Woden off-handedly. “He’ll help.”

The raven squawked, puffed up his feathers and glared indignantly at Woden.

“Now off you go, the two of you. Good luck!”

And with a sickening jolt, I found myself once more between the roots of the great oak, back to back with the sleeping Oz. But there was something pressing against my throat. Something cold, hard and sharp. I opened my eyes and saw, glinting in the moonlight, a sword. And above the sword was the mocking face of a Norman soldier.

CHAPTER TEN

Below the soldier's noseguard his mouth broke into a broad grin. His head and neck were covered by a helmet with a chain-mail hood underneath, but he didn't have any other mail on, just a leather jerkin. I saw all this in a flash and then he said something – in his own language. How was I supposed to understand him? But he wasn't talking to me. Standing over Oz was another one. My stomach clenched with fear and hatred, but I couldn't move.

A torrent of thoughts rushed through my mind and chief among them was…how could Woden let this happen? How could he send me back here with no warning? How were we supposed to complete Woden's mission if we were skewered by Norman swords?

The other soldier roared with laughter, presumably at what the first one had said, and Oz jerked awake. Then out of nowhere came a fury of black feathers, diving at the soldiers, jabbing with a massive black beak, clutching at chain-mail with talon-like claws, pecking at the Normans' eyes. Both the soldiers staggered back, raising their arms to shield their faces, and one of them dropped his sword.

That was it – the spell was broken. I rolled over, grabbed the sword and thrust it with all my might, through the leather, deep into the soldier's midriff. He teetered in mid-air before slowly collapsing backwards. Rage boiled up from my clenched stomach into my head and all my limbs. I was looking through a red haze as I twisted the sword and watched the man jerk and then lie still, blood bubbling from his mouth and seeping from his chest.

Then out of the corner of my eye I saw Oz, sword drawn, hobbling after the other soldier while the raven attacked from the air, calling his harsh battle cry.

"Don't let him go!" I yelled. I didn't care who might hear me, didn't care if there were others around. Let 'em come – I was ready for them!

Oz jabbed at the soldier and caught his arm, but he didn't do much damage. The soldier lashed back and his sword struck a glancing blow on the raven's beak. The bird squawked and paused in mid-flight, but it was enough let the man sprint away, while Oz tried in vain to catch him.

Suddenly I saw sense.

"Run!" I shouted.

"Which way?" panted Oz.

"The opposite way to him!"

We grabbed the bags and stumbled along, tripping over tree roots, scratched by brambles, deeper and deeper into the forest, with no idea where we were heading. The raven flew from branch to branch above us until Oz could go no further, even with me holding him up. We collapsed on the ground and lay gasping. The bird settled itself on a branch and closed its eyes.

I groped around for a leather bottle and when we'd both gulped down some water I looked up at the raven and smiled.

"Thank you, Muninn," I said.

"What is going on here?" panted Oz. "How comes we've suddenly got a feathered friend?"

"This is Muninn," I said, "and I've got absolutely no idea how I'm going to explain all this to you."

"It's a good name for a raven," said Oz.

"You remember it then?" I asked.

"You're kidding," said Oz. "Of course. He was one of Woden's two ravens."

"What would you say if I told you he *is* one of Woden's two ravens?"

Oz started laughing. "Oh yeah. I suppose next we'll be meeting Sleipnir, his eight-legged horse."

I frowned. "I don't think so. But this *is* Muninn."

Oz raised himself on one elbow and looked at me.

"You're serious, aren't you?"

I sat up. "Listen Oz, something really weird has happened."

"I know. We've been rescued by a raven."

"Yeah, but before that. When you went to sleep. I couldn't sleep and I was looking at this." I pulled my rune-stone out from inside my shirt. "The moon shone down on it and suddenly...I was somewhere else."

"What, like having a dream?"

"No, not like that. I was in this forest clearing with..." there was no way round this. I had to just say it. "With Woden. And I was really, really there – not dreaming."

Oz slowly sat himself up until his face was level with mine.

"If you're having me on..."

"I'm not, I promise! Look, you've always been interested in my mum's runes. You believe they can do weird things, don't you?"

Oz nodded slowly, and I told him everything that had happened in Woden's clearing.

"You're telling me that we *won* the battle...and then we lost it?"

I nodded.

"Then how comes I can't remember any of this?"

He suddenly grabbed my shirt.

"If I find you're kidding me, I'll kill you!" he said through gritted teeth. Then he let go. "At the moment I think you're having a funny turn, but if I find you're just having a laugh..."

"No, no, I've just got to find a way to make you remember." I stopped. "Muninn! You're supposed to be helping me out here."

The raven flapped down and waddled over to Mum's bag. Holding it open with one claw, he rummaged around with his beak and pulled out her little leather purse. Then he shook it and all her rune-stones fell out on to the ground. Oz watched with his mouth open as Muninn separated three runes from the others. Peorth, Mann and Wynn. I beamed at the raven.

"Muninn, you're a genius!"

Next he flew up and pulled a twig off a tree. He gave it to me and stood back expectantly.

"I get it! I have to make a bindrune!"

I cleared a small patch of earth, brushing away leaves and moss until there was a big enough space to draw on. Then I scratched a shape with the stick. First Peorth, then Mann over the first shape and finally Wynn, until a shakily drawn bindrune was scratched on to the ground. Oz's mouth was still open.

"So now what?" I asked the raven. "Does he just stare at it until something happens?"

Muninn cawed and strutted over to Oz. He glared at him fiercely and then looked at me.

"Oh, you're going to do your thing!" I said, delighted. "Right, Oz. Just stare at the bindrune."

Oz's mouth slowly closed.

"I don't know how you're doing this," he said. "Is he a trained raven or something? How did he just turn up here?"

Muninn flapped his wings and flew into Oz, knocking him over.

"No, please, Oz!" I pleaded. "Don't hurt him, Muninn! You've got to believe me, Oz! Just do it! Just stare at the bindrune!"

Oz righted himself and shot the raven a look of pure malice. But he did start to look at the shape on the ground.

"All right, all right," he grumbled. "I'm looking at it. What happens next?"

What happened next was a deafening caw from Muninn, which echoed on and on until I cowered down with my hands over my ears. Then I saw Oz's face, which was frozen in astonishment, eyes popping, mouth gaping. I must have looked like that when I was remembering, like a bit of an idiot. The noise died away and still Oz sat there unmoving, frozen, amazed.

Suddenly, he shook himself and his eyes moved from the bindrune to my face. He leaned over and grabbed hold of my shirt.

"We won!" he whispered. "We won! So how come we lost? What happened? I was in Gethin's dungeon, his temple. There was this shepherd boy and we had to change shirts and then they hanged him! He was terrified and so was I. I thought they were going to hang *me*. And then you came in and they cut my arm. My arm was bleeding and Gethin fed the runes with it, with my blood. And he cut down the corpse. That shepherd boy's corpse, and he made it speak, in this horrible voice. And you were still there and then you weren't, and neither was Gethin and... something...I don't know what...something happened. And then I was back here. What happened? *What happened next*? You've got to tell me!"

"So you believe me, don't you?" I said.

"Never mind that! Of course I believe you. I've seen it. I've been there. But for God's sake tell me how we came to lose!"

Oz was gasping for breath and I felt empty, exhausted. How could I find the words to explain? Of course...Oz hadn't gone back into the past with me. He hadn't been on that whirlwind ride through the centuries and back again. He'd probably think I could have managed better. He'd blame *me* for the Norman victory. I'd imagined that everything would be all right when Oz got his memories back, but Oz's memories were not the same as mine.

Oh Woden, I prayed, *I'm so tired. Help me get through to him how difficult it was. Help me explain it the way you explained to me.*

I propped myself against a tree while Oz curled up in a ball and started to weep. Muninn perched above, glaring balefully down at us both. Then the branch shook, there was a soft thud and *two* pairs of beady black eyes were glowering at us, *two* sturdy black shapes were hunkered down on the branch.

I felt a tiny lift of my heart. Woden must know how tough this was for me. He'd sent Huginn.

CHAPTER ELEVEN

After a while Oz sat up. He wiped his face with his sleeve and let out a long sigh. Then he shook his head.

"I just can't believe this," he whispered. "All this misery, the last two years, when we actually won." He sighed again. "We sent that bastard back where he came from, yet now he's sitting on the English throne, killing people, burning villages…I don't know…I just can't believe it."

We sat in silence for a while.

Then I said, "*You* feel bad – think how *I* must feel. I said that to Woden. I feel as if it's my fault, but he said it isn't. He said…you've got to believe this, Oz. He said I saved the world from falling to pieces. He said that when you're doing something big like that, lots of things can change."

Oz shook his head once more. "All right, tell me what happened."

He sat back against a tree opposite me and folded his arms.

"Tell me how you…saved the world."

I didn't like the way he said it. I felt we were never going to be friends again, the way we always had been, but I told him anyway, all about going back in time and the storm and the earthquake, and Gethin falling into the fiery chasm and how I was whirled back to the present and couldn't believe it when I landed in the middle of the battle and the king died and everything changed. How I couldn't believe it when Oz didn't know anything about what had happened the last few weeks. And then how *I* forgot it all as well. Woden said it was the elves who gave me something to make me forget.

"You remember the elves, don't you?" I said.

He nodded wearily.

"Well, Pooka – you remember Pooka? He warned me that funny things happen when you muck around with time." Now it was my turn to shake my head. "He was right."

The silence returned. I was desperately trying to think of something else to say, but I felt so empty, I wondered if I'd ever speak again.

Then Oz raised his eyes to the two birds.

"I suppose that's Huginn?" he said.

I nodded. Oz remembered those old stories so well. He'd always loved all that stuff.

"Well, Woden's been a fat lot of good, hasn't he?" he said bitterly. "Letting us lose the battle. I thought he was supposed to be the *god* of battle."

The ravens sat up straighter. They were obviously listening to everything we said.

"I'd be careful what you say, if I were you," I looked at them. "But anyway, I don't think gods can do everything they want. Just a lot more than humans."

"No, you're right," said Oz, looking a bit more like himself. "In the stories they're just like humans with a load of extra powers...So you actually met Woden. Twice. That's not fair. Why you?"

I was so relieved that he'd started to talk normally that I didn't mind him carping.

"Well, in the first place it's because of this rune-stone Mum gave me, which it turns out *did* belong to him, and in the second place every time I meet him he tells me I've got to do something practically impossible."

"Yeah," said Oz, "but I usually end up doing it with you, so I get all the danger without actually seeing him. Imagine telling your kids that you met the king of the gods."

I almost laughed. "You reckon we're gonna live long enough to have kids, then?"

Oz grinned back. "Course we are. Once we've got rid of that bastard sitting on the English throne."

"I...no, Oz...didn't I tell you that bit?"

His smile faded. "What bit?"

"I thought I told you, but it was a lot to take in. Or perhaps I didn't."

I paused, while Oz's smile completely vanished and he stared at me coldly.

"This isn't gonna be anything good, is it?" he said.

I shook my head.

"No. He said...Woden said that this war is lost, but that England will gradually recover, but not...but probably not in our lifetime."

I waited. I waited for the anger simmering inside him to boil over and scald me, but he just sat there. His eyes went dead, and he shut them. *Then* it came.

"What!?" he yelled. "You mean all this was a waste of time? We might as well have run for the hills and hidden away? All these people dying?"

"They'd have died anyway!" I shouted back. "Or other people would have! It's good that we tried, Oz, but it's not gonna work! It's not gonna work – Woden said so!"

Suddenly the two ravens flapped down. Huginn marched up and down in front of Oz, never taking his little black eyes off him, while Muninn squawked at me. I'd never be able to understand their language the way Woden could but I was beginning to guess what Muninn was trying to tell me.

"Yes, all right, Muninn, the thing we've got to do. All right. We've got to get on with finding the rune-stones."

Oz couldn't help but look at Huginn strutting up and down in front of him. He started to say something, but Huginn cawed and interrupted him. Then the bird stood beside him and butted Oz with his head, trying to push him in my direction. Oz resisted, but Huginn wouldn't stop. Whenever Oz tried to move in a different direction, the raven barred his way, and every time he opened his mouth to speak Huginn cawed loudly.

I scrambled over and crouched in front of Oz.

"Listen, Oz, we've got to find this castle – Gethin's castle. We're wasting time." Both ravens nodded their heads up and down like mad. "Woden said it's more important than fighting a losing battle against the Normans. He said Gethin's got someone trying to get the runes and then he could use them to do something terrible – Gethin, I mean – even though he's dead."

The ravens cawed and nodded again. Oz stopped trying to move but did have one more go at saying something. This time Huginn let him. He ignored me and looked at the birds.

"All right," he said, then took a deep breath. "All right. But you've got to admit this is a lot to expect. To expect us just to give up what we've strained every bit of ourselves to do these last two years."

He was still talking to the ravens as if I wasn't there, but I was glad. Thank God Oz loved those stories about the gods. It was easier for him to accept all this than it would have been for some people.

"I'd like to meet your master," he went on, and both ravens listened with their heads on one side. "I've got a few questions I'd like to ask about why he couldn't have given us a bit more help. It seems like it's always *us* doing things for *him*."

Huginn stood up straight and his neck feathers started to fluff out, so he looked as though he was wearing a ruff.

"Oz, be careful!" I warned.

"All right, all right, I don't mean to be rude. I just wanted to get that off my chest."

I shook my head. I'd never have dared talk like that.

Huginn still looked angry, but Muninn put his head next to his brother's and cawed softly to him. The ruff round Huginn's neck slowly smoothed itself down.

Oz carried on. "I'm sure your master knows a lot of stuff that we don't, so I suppose it's right to do what he asks and try to get those rune-stones back." Both ravens nodded. "But after that, I can't see me giving up the fight. I don't know about Wulf."

For the first time he looked at me. I smiled and joined in the nodding.

"But we haven't got a clue where this castle is," he said.

Good point.

Huginn cawed loudly and flew to a branch some way away. Muninn looked at his brother, then at us, then once again at Huginn.

"I think we've got to follow them, Oz," I said.

Then Muninn cawed and flew off to join Huginn. So we gathered our things together and wearily set off after them.

And they were good guides, those birds. They skirted round any sign of Normans and found places for us to camp. They even drove gamebirds towards us, mostly grouse and partridge, so we ate quite well the next few days. Of course, we all shared the food. That meant there was never much left, because as well as helping themselves to the bits we wanted the ravens scoffed all the bits we definitely didn't want. Raw birds' gizzard has never been one of my favourites. Even when me or Oz had shot the prey without any help from Huginn and Muninn, they still demanded first pick. They tore into the carcasses, ripping at the entrails, pecking out the eyes and tossing them in the air before catching them in their beaks and swallowing them. Only then were we allowed to pluck, spit and roast the bloody remains they had left us.

Sometimes we trekked through woodland, sometimes over open fields, once or twice we even took the roads. But we never met a soul. One or other of the ravens often flew so high we could hardly see him, so I suppose that's how they knew which places to avoid. The land gradually became more hilly and one morning we could see a whole range of hills quite close.

As Oz and me were eating our cold breakfast the ravens had their heads together, muttering softly. Then they both looked at us. When they had our attention they looked at the hills and cawed loudly. They looked at us again and then repeated the process.

"Is that where we're going?" I asked. "Is that where Gethin's castle is?"

Both birds nodded.

"Is it easy to find?" said Oz.

They nodded again. Then they strutted over and walked in a circle round us both, nodding and cawing softly. Oh God, this looked horribly like goodbye, and we'd come to depend on them so much.

First Huginn and then Muninn took to the air and circled round, higher and higher, turning somersaults as they flew, dancing round each other.

"They're showing off," said Oz with half a smile.

But it was a sad smile. He knew as well.

Then the ravens soared so high that they were tiny specks in the cloudy sky. And then they were gone.

We were on our own.

CHAPTER TWELVE

We scattered the ashes of last night's fire, put a few bits of cold meat in a bag and set off. It was open moorland between us and the hills, with not a soul in sight, so we made as straight a line as we could towards them. Neither of us said anything, though I bet Oz was thinking the same as me. What was going to meet us when we found the castle? So far all I'd been thinking of was getting there.

By midday we didn't seem to have made much progress. The hills were obviously further away than they looked. We came across a little stream so we refilled our flasks and ate some cold grouse.

"It seems ages since I had a bit of bread," said Oz.

"It's not that long," I said, "it's just that such a lot has happened. Anyway, better get used to it. God knows when we'll have bread again. And this meat won't last much longer." I sat up and scanned the moors. "What creatures d'you think live round here?"

Oz shrugged and we chewed in silence. Then, turning my eyes to the hills I spied a movement, something galloping our way. But it didn't look like anything we could eat.

"Look, Oz, what's that?"

And then I could see. It was a man on horseback, making much faster progress *away* from the hills than *we* were, going towards them. I really wished we had horses.

"Duck down!" said Oz. "We don't know who it is!"

"There's nowhere to hide," I answered, "and there's only one of him."

"No, you're right," nodded Oz. "Just get our swords out and be ready for him."

So we stood for a bit with our swords drawn, and watched. From his billowing cape and flying dark hair we knew he wasn't a Norman soldier.

A tiny bit of me hoped this was someone sent by Woden. I thought back two years, to when we'd met Abdul. He'd seemed like an enemy at first, but then turned out to be a really good friend. Still, best be careful.

I couldn't get over how fast that horse was galloping. As they got closer I could see that far from urging his steed on, the rider looked as if he was hanging on for dear life and trying to slow it down.

We got well out of the way as they approached the brook. The horse jumped clear but stumbled as it landed, and the rider was thrown. But the horse wasn't hurt and as soon as it righted itself it carried on its mad, headlong dash, leaving its rider cursing on the ground. At least, I assumed he was cursing. I couldn't understand what he said, though it didn't sound like that Norman language. I had a feeling it might be Welsh.

We approached him warily, still with our swords drawn but not sure whether he was friend or enemy.

"Are you all right?" I asked. Bit of a stupid question when he'd just lost his horse, but I meant, was he injured.

He looked at me and his expression changed. Mine too, I expect, because...I knew him.

My gut clenched.

I knew him from those memories that Woden had helped me get back. Pale skin, high cheekbones, shoulder-length dark hair. This was the man who'd given Guthrum that letter we'd been told to deliver. The letter that would have been our death warrant if we'd actually managed to deliver it. And this was the man who'd opened the door to me, the door leading to Gethin's dungeon, with the skulls around the walls and the shepherd boy's corpse hanging in the middle. Both times he'd smiled at me, a smile of pleasure at the thought of the terrible things that were going to happen to me. But he wasn't smiling now.

"You!" he hissed, in English, as he staggered up from the ground.

Then I saw Oz's lip curl and his eyes narrow as he pointed his sword at the rider. Of course. Oz had been in that dungeon. What was *he* remembering? He'd been forced to change clothes with the young shepherd and then had to watch as the terrified boy was hanged. What part this man had played in all that I didn't know, but he'd been there so

I could make a good guess. He drew his own sword and walked towards me with fury written all over his face.

"Watch it!" Oz hissed at him. "There's two of us, you may have noticed."

The man stopped and gave Oz a contemptuous glance before turning back to me. Then his sword arm dropped to his side and he gave a manic kind of laugh and once he'd started he couldn't seem to stop. Oz and I looked at each other and took a few more steps towards him, swords at the ready. But it was off-putting, the way he stood there laughing. Had he gone mad?

And then Oz lunged. Quick as lightning the rider dodged out of the way, but I attacked from the other side. He parried my stroke and retreated a few steps.

"Oh, yes. There are two of you," he panted, his eyes darting from me to Oz and back again. "And one of you," pointing the sword at me, "caused the death of my master. But not on your own. You couldn't have. So who was helping you?" All the while he was talking he was backing away from us. "Who told you what to do? I think I can guess. But those runes are *ours* now and they will bring my master back to life!"

What!?

So that's what we had to stop! We *had* to get to them before he did! But why had he been galloping *away* from the castle, away from the runes?

Oz was edging towards him, his face twisted with hatred, but the man carried on backing away.

"I won't bother to fight you now," he went on, "when a far worse fate awaits you beyond those hills. I would love to see your faces when you get there."

He put the fingers of his free hand to his lips and whistled and Oz took the chance to lunge again. But this man was quick. He deflected the blow and struck back. Now he'd stopped laughing I joined in and I think me and Oz would have got the better of him but for the horse.

It came galloping back, flanks shiny with sweat, and charged straight at me. I barely managed to jump out of the way before it wheeled round and cantered up to its master, who flung himself up on its back. Then it neighed, turned to Oz and reared up on its hind legs. Oz scrambled out of the way of the flailing hooves and the rider started laughing again. Then he rode the wild-eyed horse up and down in front of us.

"You see my horse, how brave he is?" he called. "He has never run from danger. Never. But did you see how panic-stricken he was just now, how he fled in terror? How brave are you? *I* will devise a plan. I will find those runes. But *you*, poor dolts, what is in store for you at my master's castle?"

Then he galloped away while I stood there like an idiot. But Oz wasn't finished. He didn't have a spear, so bellowing like a berserker he flung his sword at the rider. It fell short and Oz stood with clenched fists, breathing heavily, as horse and rider got smaller and smaller, further and further away until they vanished into the distance.

At last Oz spoke, his voice coming out in a strangled croak. "He killed him, that poor kid. Him and Gethin, they strung him up and he was terrified. And so was I. I thought they were going to do the same to me."

I walked over and put a hand on his shoulder. There was nothing I could say. I could barely imagine it.

Then he gulped in some air and went on in a more normal voice. "He was just trying to frighten us, then. He went to get the runes and it was a bit harder than he thought it was going to be, so he's going to get some help and he wanted to scare us. He was trying to put us off going."

"I don't think so, Oz. I've never seen a horse look that scared. What have we let ourselves in for?"

"I know," he sighed. "I was only trying to cheer us up a bit."

Oz was himself again. Suddenly, all the bad feeling that had been hanging around vanished into thin air. He was my friend once more (I'd never stopped being his) and things were back to how they used to be. Which was great except that we'd got to go and face some horrific unknown danger and probably get ourselves killed.

"Right," I said. "I vote we go as far as we can today without crossing those hills and then face up to whatever it is in the morning."

So we did. Oz went to get his sword back, then we walked on for a few hours, set up camp in a hollow as the ground started to rise, and ate our cold meat. We didn't dare light a fire in case the smoke attracted who knows what, so we slept back to back for warmth. Though I'm not sure either of us got much sleep.

"Let's get it over with," I said as the sun rose behind us, and we clambered upwards. After a while we both became aware of a low rumbling noise. It started and stopped, started and stopped, rhythmically, like something breathing.

"Oh my God, it's a giant," whispered Oz.

"It can't be," I whispered back. "There's no such things."

"Yeah, like there's no such things as gods and elves," said Oz.

I'd known it was a stupid thing to say even when I was saying it. Oz was right. We knew from experience that the world was full of wonders… and horrors.

"Let's go really slowly and quietly," I whispered. "Don't send any stones flying. It sounds like something sleeping and we don't want to wake it up, whatever it is."

So the last bit of the climb took forever, as we struggled over rocks and scree as stealthily as we could. At last we reached what seemed to be the very top, held our breath and peered over.

"Oh my God," whispered Oz.

CHAPTER THIRTEEN

The sun was now just high enough to shine on the west side of the hills and its morning rays were gleaming on something red gold. Something vast with two nostrils the size of rabbit holes, out of which came puffs of smoke in time with the rumbling noise. Something scaly, with two huge webbed wings folded flat along its back and crooked legs tucked underneath it in its slumber. Its long, long body and spiked tail were coiled around a stone-built castle. The castle we were supposed to enter, to get Woden's runes for him.

I'd imagined all kinds of things since seeing that terrified horse. Demons guarding the entrance, magical fire impossible to pass, even Oz's giant. But I'd never imagined a dragon.

"Oh my God," whispered Oz again.

I said nothing. I slumped down to the ground unsure whether to laugh or cry. Woden must have known. What was he playing at? Oz lowered himself down beside me with a dazed expression as if someone had hit him on the head.

"No wonder that horse went berserk," he said.

"Keep your voice down," I muttered.

"D'you reckon dragons have got good ears?" he whispered back.

"I don't know, but there's no point risking it."

After a while of just sitting there, I said, "I wonder if there's any way we could sneak in, round the back perhaps, without him knowing."

"It might not be a him," said Oz. "Suppose it's a her and she's got eggs inside the castle, that she's guarding till they hatch into lots of little baby dragons."

I shot him a filthy look. "I suppose *that's* meant to cheer us up as well."

He shrugged and we stood up and peered over again. And once more I was hit by the sheer vastness of the creature, curled all the way around the castle, but also by its terrible beauty. Its scales gleamed in the sun, sometimes gold, sometimes copper, and its even breathing showed a creature completely relaxed in a peaceful slumber. For who could dare to disturb it?

Suddenly it yawned, sucking in air so that nearby trees bent towards it as if blown by a wind. Then it stretched out its forelegs, like a cat waking from sleep. Its claws and teeth were like curved swords, and as it breathed out, flames shot from its cavern of a mouth. The ground in front of it was already scorched black. Then it shifted its great head slightly, tucked its legs underneath again and settled itself back to sleep.

Oz pulled me down.

"This is completely hopeless," he whispered. "You know that, don't you?"

"It can't be," I said. "Woden wouldn't have asked us to do something impossible."

"Oh no?" said Oz. "You notice he pulled his precious ravens out of it before we got here. I reckon he thinks we're stupid enough to give this a go and if we get burnt to a crisp it's no big deal to him. He'll just think of some other way to get his runes back."

I stared at him. I couldn't believe that. If I didn't have faith in Woden who could I have faith in? Besides, Oz hadn't met him. He hadn't felt the power in that glade in the forest, the awe that I'd felt as I'd recognized the Allfather, chief of all the gods.

"He's not called the Allfather for nothing," I said. "He's not just a king, he's meant to be like everyone's father as well."

Oz raised his eyebrows. "You reckon your dad would have made you fight a dragon? Your dad tried to *save* your life when you were facing those monsters and he died while he was doing it. Remember?"

"Shut up, Oz!" I said, before I thought to keep my voice down. I had enough to deal with without dredging up those memories and all the complicated feelings that went with them.

"Look," I whispered. "It can't be impossible. If we walk round till we get to a gap in the hills – there was one, I saw it – we can creep through and see if there's a way in without disturbing it. There might be a tunnel or something that we can't see from here."

"I think you're mad," said Oz, "but I'm not gonna leave you here to try on your own."

"Thanks, Oz."

"But you've got to promise me," he went on, "that when it's obvious we can't do anything without committing suicide – and I think that's obvious now – you'll give up."

"It just can't be impossible," I said again. "But yeah, thanks."

So we clambered carefully down the steep bit of the hill and began to trudge northwards to where I was sure I'd seen an easier way into the valley. We didn't talk much at first but then Oz started to go on about how this was ridiculous and we'd be much better off trying to find our men and rejoin the fight. I put up with it for a while, but by the time we were nearing the pass through the hills I'd had enough. I stopped dead and put my bag down.

"Look, Oz," I snapped. "You heard what that rider said, about needing to find the runes to bring his master back to life?"

Oz gave a grudging nod.

"Well, Gethin was a massively powerful magician and he hated the English. If he came back, not only would *we* be dead meat, you and me personally, but he'd do everything in his power to help the Normans beat the whole English nation. *And* perhaps plunge the whole world into chaos."

"Yeah," muttered Oz, as light finally dawned in his not always brilliant head. I don't mean he was thick. Not at all. But he didn't stop to think things through.

"So the best thing we can do to help our side win," I went on, "is to get to those rune-stones before Gethin's man does. Get it?"

He got it.

"Yeah, sorry, you're right," he grinned.

One of the good things about Oz is, he never really bears a grudge. He might carry on a bit as if he does, but he doesn't mean it. I didn't remind him that Woden said the Normans were going to win because perhaps he wouldn't care about the rest of the world if the English lost.

So on we went until an opening appeared, a sort of gash in the hillside, leading to the valley with the castle. And the dragon. We couldn't see it – the dragon I mean – because the path wasn't straight, but we could hear it again. Rumble, rumble as it breathed in its sleep. We both reckoned we were some way from its head now, but still we crept as quietly as we could down the path. We passed a cave on either side, one large – home to wolves perhaps – and one quite small. The bigger one looked promising. We should come back to that.

Then rounding a corner we saw, some yards away, that the path ended in a wall. A huge scaly wall that went in and out in time with the rumbling. We jumped back, but luckily didn't make any noise. There was a faint smell about, not a nice one, which reminded me of something, I couldn't think what.

"So where's your tunnel into the castle?" whispered Oz.

"I didn't say there *was* one," I hissed back. "I just said there *might* be. That cave looked possible. But let's get a bit closer."

We crept forward until we reached the end of the path…hoping for a way we could edge round the dragon? Hoping to suddenly come across a door marked *secret passage*? Hoping for a miracle. But there was nothing. The dragon seemed to have wedged itself right up against the hillside.

Time to investigate the cave.

I pointed towards it, Oz nodded and we crept back the way we'd come. Inside, it smelled damp and earthy, but there was no strong animal stink. Nonetheless we trod carefully. Of course, after a few steps we couldn't see a thing.

"Hang on, I'll find my flint," said Oz and we went back to the cave mouth. I stood outside with him, breathing in that faintly familiar smell while he put his bag down and rummaged around among our few remaining bits of meat. When he pulled out the flint, the first thing he did was drop it and it bounced against the rock wall, setting off a little fall of stones.

We froze. There was silence. Silence where there should have been the rumble of the dragon's breathing. A shadow fell on us and we raised our eyes in horror.

CHAPTER FOURTEEN

A great scaly head was rearing up into the sky. Its eyes were open, golden eyes with black slits, once again reminding me of a monstrous cat. The head turned in our direction.

"Get inside!" I yelled, and we dived for the cave entrance. There was an almighty roar and we felt a fierce heat on our backs as we raced further into the cave. In a sudden flare of light we could see the cave walls and each other's faces, distorted in terror. Then blackness again, a pause, and then more roaring, another flash of light as flames filled the passage through the hills, scorching everything in their path while we crouched in horror.

And then silence. And the smell. It had grown much stronger in the fiery blast and I knew now what it reminded me of. Rotten eggs.

I don't know how long we stayed there, curled up, afraid to move. At last I heard a sob, and realized it came from my own mouth. I tried to stifle the noise, but I couldn't stop the spasms shaking my body. I couldn't stop the tears dripping off the end of my nose.

It was all too much. Mum killing herself. Finding out all the things that had happened that we'd forgotten about. The painful knowledge that we'd won the battle against the Normans, and then we'd lost it. Woden giving us this impossible thing to do.

I felt an arm round my shoulder.

"Don't worry, mate," whispered Oz. "We'll get through this."

I didn't answer.

"Tell you what," he went on. "Why don't we explore a bit more? You've got a flint in your bag too, haven't you, but…better not try that again. We can just feel our way, see if it leads anywhere."

I listened amazed. This was the Oz who thought it was all useless and we'd be better off trying to find our men. He'd actually got me to promise we'd do that if everything looked hopeless, and I didn't think it could look much more hopeless than this. At that moment I loved him, my best friend, the brother I'd never had.

"All right, thanks," I whispered, and we stood up and started to feel our way round the walls of the cave. There were no animals there – I couldn't blame them for not wanting to be that close to the dragon – but there wasn't anything else either. We soon found ourselves back where we started.

"We might as well go," I whispered, but neither of us moved.

"I don't think I'm going anywhere till I'm good and certain that thing's asleep," said Oz, and I nodded, though he couldn't see me. So we sat down and waited. We waited for a long, long time. Then we shuffled a bit closer to the entrance and listened.

The dragon was sleeping. We could hear the rumble of its deep untroubled breathing, as if it had been woken by the buzzing of a fly and had sunk once again into pleasant dreams. But still we didn't move.

At last I whispered, "We should go now. It might wake up in a minute and stay awake for ages."

Oz looked at me and gingerly stepped out into the open. At his feet was a blackened pile of cinders – the remains of his bag with our last scraps of food. We listened again. The breathing continued. I followed Oz and at last we made our way painfully slowly back down the pathway. We passed the other cave, but it was so small we'd have had to wriggle on our stomachs to get inside and all we wanted was to get away.

After who knew how long of watching where we put our feet and hardly daring to breathe, of looking back in the dread of seeing that massive head glaring down at us, we reached the end of the path. Still trying to be quiet, we walked away towards the edge of a forest, the first woods we'd seen for quite a while.

And then we ran.

We ran until Oz started to limp again, though his leg had been so much better since we'd been with the ravens. I was out of breath anyway and we'd put some distance between us and the hills. The forest looked safe, untouched by dragon-fire and it was an easy walk away now. All I wanted to do was reach the trees, curl up and go to sleep. I was bone tired. But Oz seemed to have a new lease of life despite his limp.

"I'm starving!" he said. "That dragon slightly overcooked what was left of our meat, but there's probably some game in the wood."

And then we both stopped in our tracks. On the open moorland near the trees sat a hare. It was gazing up at something. I looked up and saw a sliver of moon in the sky, although it wasn't yet dark. The sun was setting behind the hills and I caught my breath when I looked back and noticed for the first time a rosy glow in the sky. Streaks of pink blended with pale green, which turned into blue. Not yet the dark blue of night, but a soft, gentle blue like a duck's egg. It lifted me up out of myself and my misery. *There's so much beauty in the world*, the sunset told me. *Your troubles are nothing. They will pass.*

I looked again at the hare, gazing not at the sunset but at the thin crescent moon on the other side of the sky. It was a lovely creature, smooth grey-brown fur, long ears coloured pink by the light shining through them. Then I felt Oz moving stealthily beside me. He was nocking an arrow to his bowstring, as noiselessly as he could. I hesitated. How could we kill it? But how could we go on if we didn't have something to eat? Memories of my mum's stewed hare made my stomach rumble. "All life feeds on other life," she used to say, so I reluctantly readied my bow as well.

But just as we pulled back our bowstrings a figure stepped out of the wood. A slender young woman, not much more than a girl, with black plaits down to her waist and a basket over her arm.

"No, don't!" she cried.

I dropped my bow, while Oz let an arrow fly. But the hare was speeding away on its long legs and the arrow thudded uselessly into the ground.

I stared at the girl. I just couldn't believe my eyes.

"Bronwen!" I gasped.

CHAPTER FIFTEEN

"What did you do that for?" yelled Oz, before he twigged who it was. Then he gaped. "My God! Bron! What are you doing here?"

She was the only one of us who didn't look surprised.

"I could ask you the same question," she said, smiling. "This isn't so far from my home, you know, but a long way from yours. And I've had a feeling you might turn up."

She walked towards us and I couldn't think of a single thing to say, but I felt myself grinning foolishly.

"Home?" sighed Oz. "I've forgotten what that is."

"I know," said Bronwen. "You've suffered. I have a little hut in the woods and a basket full of mushrooms. Come and have supper with me."

I was in a dream, but Oz wasn't.

"So I'm asking you again," he said. "What did you do that for?"

"She was moon-gazing – the hare – and it didn't seem right. Besides, it's Friday."

She turned and beckoned for us to follow.

"Friday!" said Oz. "What's that got to do with it?"

"I still keep the church's rules, more or less," said Bronwen, "though the church seems to have given up on me."

"So we can't eat a bit of meat because it's Friday!" erupted Oz. "After all we've been through...practically been roasted by a dragon. I bet that dragon didn't care that it was Friday!"

I couldn't help laughing, and Bronwen turned and smiled at me. We were almost under the trees by now and I stopped to have one more look at the sunset.

"Yes, it's beautiful, isn't it," said Bron.

"Friday!" muttered Oz.

"Come on," said Bron. "I've got a pot with some stewed vegetables. We can add the mushrooms and heat it up."

"Yeah, that would have gone really well with stewed hare," said Oz bitterly.

For the first time Bronwen showed some annoyance.

"You haven't changed much, Osric, have you?" she said. "With everything you've been through I thought you might have grown up a bit."

"How do *you* know what I've been through?" Oz demanded. "I'm a man now, a soldier! Don't tell *me* to grow up!"

The two of them glared at each other, Bronwen frowning, Oz with flared nostrils, both of them up for a fight.

It was just like old times. That's what broke my trance.

"Why don't you pick up a branch and whack him, Bron?" I grinned. "Like you did that other time."

They looked at me surprised and then we all burst out laughing.

"That was when Abdul was with us, wasn't it?" she said, beaming at me. "And we were looking for a story to explain why we were travelling together, and Oz was trying to get us to pretend I was his young bride."

"Yeah," said Oz. "Good old Abdul. Wonder what happened to him."

Then his expression changed as he realized what had struck me straight away.

"You remember, Bron!" I gasped. "But how? You remember what happened!"

"Some of it," she nodded. "A lot of bits and pieces, but I can't fit them all together. Perhaps you can help."

"Perhaps we can," I said, gazing at her. My heart, which had been full of despair at our failure to get into the castle, was now floating upwards like those rosy clouds in the sky.

She turned and entered the forest. "Let's go home and have something to eat, and then we can talk about it."

"Yeah, home," said Oz. "That'd be nice. And so would something to eat."

Bronwen's home turned out to be an old hermit's hut a little way into the woods.

"It's got everything I need," she said. "A roof over my head, a cooking pot and a stream nearby. I've even got a bed, though you two will have to sleep on the floor over there. We can make it comfortable with dry grass and I've got an extra cover."

"We've had a lot worse," said Oz.

Wood for a fire was already in a neat pile outside the hut, so it didn't take long to light. An old iron pot was dangling over it, full of chopped-up vegetables already partly stewed. Bronwen washed the mushrooms in the stream and added them to the mix. Meanwhile Oz and I had a quick wash and made a mattress of dried grass in the opposite corner from Bron's bed. Though in truth it wasn't very far from it, the hut was so small.

"Where d'you get the veg?" said Oz.

"I still have some friends in the village," said Bronwen, "though the priest isn't very fond of me now. There's a little vegetable patch out the back, but I'm afraid I've let it go. I didn't think I'd be here very long. The hermit was a friend and when he became too frail to stay here he went back to his abbey and said I could use the hut for a while."

We sat round the fire talking while the food cooked and homely smells wafted up our nostrils.

"So how comes you remember things that everyone else has forgotten?" asked Oz, but I thought I knew.

"Well, I didn't at first," said Bronwen. "When the Normans took over we came back to Wales, Lady Rhiannon and me. I was so glad we did. Nain was ill and my lady released me from her service so I could look after her. What a blessing. We had a few months together before she died and I learnt so much from her. She had a peaceful end."

I stared into the flames.

"My mum died as well," I said, "but it wasn't...like that."

I pictured Bronwen's grandmother coming quietly to the end of her natural life and then I unsuccessfully tried to block the image of Mum plunging the knife into her own midriff. When I looked up I found Bron gazing at me with a half-smile half-frown and wondered how much she knew.

"So, Bron, when did you start to remember?" persisted Oz.

"It was dreams at first, after Nain died, and I thought that's all they were. But I soon realized…You know, I've always had some second sight, and so did Nain, but I couldn't always make out what it was trying to tell me. I'm better at it now and I realized these dreams really happened. But let's talk about that later…supper is ready!"

She went into the hut and came out with bowls, spoons and a ladle, which she flourished triumphantly.

"The hermit wasn't a complete solitary," she explained. "Lucky for us, he liked to have visitors."

There wasn't much talking for a while. The meal was delicious, even without the stewed hare, and me and Oz were starving.

Bronwen carried on talking while we both had second helpings.

"You asked about Abdul," she said, "and that's strange, because I remember two different things about him. I remember him dying after Gethin wounded him."

We both stopped eating and looked at her.

"You remember when Gethin cast that spell and we were all paralysed?" she said. "He carted you off, Wulfstan, and I think you, Osric, must have already been captured by him."

Oz nodded.

"But he left Abdul and me on the hillside. Only, before he left he thrust his sword into Abdul's side. When we came back to life the wound was bleeding," she shook her head, "such a lot of blood. I managed to get him on to his horse and we rode to a shepherd's hut, but he couldn't go any further. I had to leave him and ride on to the abbey on my own. I wanted to fetch Brother Walter – you remember him?"

We both nodded this time.

"I thought he could heal him, but it was too late. Just after we reached the hut Abdul died." She paused. "I was heartbroken."

I sat up and looked hard at Bronwen. Abdul was a good friend to all of us, but the way she said it, it sounded like something more. Had she fallen in love with Abdul? Oz was looking stunned as well, but for a slightly different reason. Neither of us had had any idea that Abdul was dead and that in itself was a shock.

"Walter took me back to the abbey and I think now that I stayed there a few days, but then suddenly I was back with Lady Rhiannon and I had no memory of any of that – Abdul, Walter, Gethin. Nothing. And there was panic everywhere because the Normans had won the battle. I don't understand this, because the English had won, hadn't they, but at that time I didn't remember that. And my lady's husband was killed in the battle. So we got on a cart with her baby and rode back home. But… this is the really strange thing. On the way we passed Abdul on his black horse, riding in the opposite direction. And we both looked at each other for a long time as we passed, as if we knew each other, but we didn't. And at this time I had no memory of him dying, or any of those other things that happened. Only much later did I realize that the man in black, on the black horse, was my Abdul, *our* Abdul. So he died, but he came to life again." She sighed. "Can you help me to understand all this? And how is it that *you* remember? You don't have second sight, do you?"

So between us we told her about my journey hundreds of years into the past and how I didn't arrive back in the present at exactly the same time as when I left and how Woden and his ravens helped us get our memories back. It took a long time to tell all this and as we finished it was quite dark. Outside our little circle of firelight the night was pitch black.

"And the last thing we needed," said Oz, rounding off the story, "was a dragon! We got to the castle, with Woden's runes in, and this flipping dragon nearly roasted us!"

"Oh, dear," said Bronwen. "You must have done something to upset her."

I smiled but Oz burst out laughing.

"No, I'm not joking," said Bron. "She's quite sweet-tempered if you talk to her nicely."

We gaped at her.

"The trouble is, she's a Welsh dragon, and I don't think she speaks English."

CHAPTER SIXTEEN

I sat there with my mouth open but a grin slowly spread across Oz's face.

"Nice one, Bron," he said. "So you go and talk to her politely in Welsh and she'll let us into the castle?"

"Quite possibly," said Bronwen seriously. "I don't see why not."

I was totally confused. She didn't seem to be messing around. But she had to be!

Oz laughed. "All right, all right, very funny."

An owl hooted and I was suddenly aware of the surrounding blackness. Bronwen shook her head. As if reading my mind she suggested we smother the fire and go inside.

"I can wash the bowls in the morning. Let me just light a candle from the flames."

She went in the hut and came back with a sturdy tallow candle.

"Another present from the villagers?" I asked.

"No, this one's from Nain's cottage. I brought quite a bit of stuff with me."

We were soon sitting in the tiny hut, Bron on her bed and Oz and me on our grass mattress. Oz was still grinning.

"We need to have a serious talk," said Bronwen. "I'd like to know, Osric, why you find it so fantastic that I could talk to a dragon. *You've* met Woden's ravens and we've all seen all manner of things which some people wouldn't believe."

Oz's grin faded. He was starting to look a bit irritated so I jumped in.

"It's because," I explained, "this particular dragon tried to kill us. And she's *enormous* and extremely fierce! She doesn't exactly look like the sort of creature you could have a friendly chat with."

"Yeah!" said Oz. "Well put, my friend."

"So you haven't *really* talked to her," I went on. "Have you?"

Bronwen sighed. "It was talking to Tanllyd that made the priest throw me out of the village."

"Talking to who?" said Oz.

"Tanllyd," replied Bron. "It means fiery in English and I believe it's quite a common name among dragons. A bit like Bronwen for Welsh girls."

Oz held both his hands up. "Hang on, hang on. *Ha-a-ang* on. This... is...ridiculous!"

I hated to admit it, but I agreed with him. I began to wonder if Bron had gone a bit funny in the head. If we hadn't *seen* the monster, if we were talking about some baby dragon, I might have thought it possible.

Bronwen was silent for a few moments. Then she said, "I'm disappointed. You come here telling me stories about being whirled back through time, about meeting gods, about the magic power of runes, and then you don't believe me."

When she put it like that I felt a bit awkward. She didn't *seem* out of her mind apart from this dragon thing. Oz had folded his arms and looked as if he was trying to work out what on earth was going on.

"All right," I said. "Tell us what happened."

She paused. "I don't come from round here," she began. "Our village was further west and everyone loved Nain, even the priest. He knew she was a Christian even if she did have...some other powers. But then the old priest died and the new one wasn't so broad-minded. He said that using herbs and healing people was devil's work, unless you did it through the church. I told him! 'As if the devil wanted to help people!' I said. But he said the devil would use women like Nain to lure souls away from the church. Everything had to go through the priest and the sacraments. Load of rubbish! As if God's world doesn't have more in it than that."

Bron was getting really worked up just talking about it. Her cheeks had started to go pink. I was fascinated because my mum had faced a lot of prejudice and I always thought it was because she wasn't a Christian. But it seemed as if you could still get into trouble just by healing people even if you did believe in the church. How narrow-minded could you get?

"It *is* a load of rubbish," I agreed. "So what happened next?"

"So in the end we had to move. People were so sorry to see us go. And Nain was ill, but he still made us leave. He was a wicked man, that priest."

"Yeah," said Oz. "What a bastard!"

Bronwen nodded. "But Nain had some relatives in this village near here, so we walked here, very slowly, and they made us welcome. There was even a little empty hut where I could make Nain comfortable and to tell the truth that was one of the best times of my life. I'm grateful for that time, really I am."

"So why are you here, in the woods?" I asked.

She sighed. "Well, you know how word gets around, even from one valley to the next. I started to help people, doing the kind of things I'd learned from Nain. And the priest heard why we'd been thrown out before, so he began to keep a close eye on me. As if I was doing anything wrong! Though I think it might have been all right if the dragon hadn't come."

Now we really sat up. We were getting to the heart of the matter. But Bronwen didn't speak for a while. The candle flame lit up her oval face as different expressions flitted across it, mainly sad ones.

"We shouldn't use too much more of your candle," I said.

"No, it's all right," smiled Bronwen. "Usually I go to bed at sundown and get up at sunrise but this is special, isn't it? A reunion of old friends."

Yes, very special, I thought. She fell silent again.

"And?" prompted Oz at last. "So tell us about when the dragon came."

"Yes, sorry," said Bron. "Well it's strange, but Nain had been *talking* to me about dragons. This was near the end and at first I thought she was rambling. But you know she had the sight and, well, she sort of knew a dragon was coming. She'd never seen one but she'd been told a lot about them by her own mother." She paused again. "There aren't so many left in the world now, you know. They're an ancient race but they mainly speak the language of the country where they live. I think this one is very old, so she doesn't speak your language, which has only been here for a few hundred years."

Oz was starting to get that 'I don't believe this' expression on his face again, so I thought I'd better nudge Bronwen on with her story.

"So when did the dragon come?" I asked.

"Not till after Nain had died. She landed near the next village but she didn't do a *lot* of damage. Ate a few sheep, accidentally burnt part of an orchard. But she curled up and went to sleep right next to where people lived, and she didn't look as if she was going to move in a hurry. Obviously there was total panic and our village was flooded with incomers who we had to feed and shelter. There was talk of finding a hero to kill her – only they didn't know she was a her. The priest said she'd been sent by the devil because people hadn't been obeying God's laws."

"He would," I said.

Bron smiled at me. "So then I volunteered to go and talk to her."

"You what?" said Oz.

"Nain had told me the way to talk to a dragon. You must bow and be very respectful, say, 'O ancient one,' and stuff like that. If you approach them openly, with no weapons, they'll listen to you. Obviously don't go near if they're on the rampage. Just wait till they're quiet. So that's what I did."

"My God!" I gasped. "Weren't you terrified?"

"I was, yes. My clothes were sticking to me, I was wet with fear. She was so...big, and so...she looked as if she came from another world. But when I looked into her eyes, somehow...there was someone there – a sort of connection between us. Also I felt – this will sound silly – but I felt that Nain was with me."

Oz's expression had completely changed. He obviously believed Bron and it looked as if his admiration for her had shot up to the sky. Mine certainly had, though I had a pretty high opinion of her to start with.

"What on earth did you say to her?" he asked, amazed.

"I asked her name and told her mine and said how magnificent she was. They're a bit vain, dragons. Then I asked how long she was going to stay there. She hadn't decided, and I explained that she was stopping a lot of people from getting on with their lives, and of course all those people also thought she was magnificent and were honoured that she was there."

I laughed. "You don't have to tell the truth to a dragon, then?"

"Well no, not when you're flattering them. But I wondered if she wouldn't like to find somewhere quieter to sleep and said there were lots of valleys around with no villages in. She thought about that and said she'd fly around and have a look. She'd been in a cave for a long time and wanted to be in the open air. So she went off flying for a while and I just waited. All the villagers had been hiding, wanting to know what was going on and the priest was looking daggers at me. When they saw her in the distance, coming back, they ran.

"And Tanllyd told me she'd found a nice deserted valley with a castle where no-one lived any more, which would suit her very well. I bowed and thanked her but I did ask if she'd be raiding the area, looking for food. She said she didn't need to eat very often, which is surprising, isn't it, for a great creature like that. But she said as I'd been so friendly she'd try and vary the places she hunted and not disturb us too much. And then she flew off."

"So it's actually *your* fault," said Oz, "that she's wrapped herself around the very castle that we need to get into."

"Shut up, Oz!" I hissed. That was all we needed, another bit of Oz v Bron warfare.

Luckily Bron found it funny. "Oh, Osric," she laughed. "We're just going to have to get used to each other, aren't we?"

He grinned. Then he said, "But what have *you* got, to make her so pally with you when she tried to fry us? Why couldn't she be friendly with us?"

"Perhaps because you were sneaking up on her from behind? You do have to approach them carefully."

"And I still don't understand," I frowned, "why you're here, in this wood."

"The priest accused me of being a witch," she said simply, "in league with the devil's creatures."

"My God," I said. "You'd think he'd have been grateful."

She nodded. "Everyone else was. It was lucky that I'd made friends with Llewyn, the dear old hermit, and that he was going back to his abbey and he let me come here."

"So how exactly," said Oz thoughtfully, "can you help us?"

"Well," said Bron, "I'd like to know exactly why your Woden needs his runes back so badly."

"Because they're really powerful," I answered, "and they're just lying around in the castle and if Gethin's man gets to them before we do he can bring Gethin back to life and then God knows what'll happen. But nothing good."

Bronwen sighed. "He was an evil man. When I think what he did to Abdul. And if he comes back to life he'll be even more full of anger and hatred."

"Yeah," said Oz, "exactly. So really, we need to get going on it."

"On what?" I asked. "You're not really gonna go and talk to that monster are you?"

I was suddenly filled with horror at the thought of Bronwen, who I'd only just found again, standing in front of the dragon and being burnt to a cinder. Suppose the dragon wasn't in such a good mood this time. Suppose she had had a few sheep to eat before, but she was hungry now and fancied a nice Bronwen-sized snack.

"No!" I shouted. "There must be another way!"

Bron shook her head. "Well, we could wait around a few hundred years before she decides to move on," she said. "Don't be silly, Wulfstan. I'll ask her to let you into the castle. It's the only way."

"And the sooner the better," said Oz.

"Tomorrow," said Bronwen. "We'll do it tomorrow."

CHAPTER SEVENTEEN

The next morning I didn't feel any better about it. It was a bit of a trek to the valley opening where the castle gate was. And the dragon's head. All the while we were walking I was racking my brains to think of another way of doing this. I'd been so down, so low when we couldn't get into the castle, but then I'd seen the sunset, which had lifted me up out of myself. And then we'd met Bron. She'd appeared like a figure out of a story and reminded me that there are good things in the world. It wasn't all fighting and misery. It might be possible to have a happy life.

And now she was going to offer herself up to a dragon. It was madness to think the dragon would be as friendly this time as it'd been before. I didn't think I could bear to lose her when I'd just found her.

"Are you sure, Bron," I asked, "that you couldn't just teach me the words to say to the dragon? I'm a quick learner." I wasn't sure that was true. The only other language I'd tried to learn had been a bit of church Latin, and I hadn't been all that brilliant at it.

"Oh Wulfstan, we've been through all this," she sighed. "Even if you could learn a little speech in this short time, you wouldn't have a clue what she was saying when she answered you. You couldn't have a conversation. And Tanllyd knows me. She knows I don't mean any harm, but she just might recognize you as someone who tried to sneak up on her from behind."

"She's right, Wulf," said Oz cheerfully, as if we were going on a jolly day out instead of to our possible doom. "And you were the one who was so dead set on getting these runes back. Woden charged *you*, remember?"

"Of course I remember!" I said tetchily. "I just don't like putting Bron in danger."

"That's sweet of you," she smiled at me. "But there's no other way, so let's hear no more of it."

We trudged on in silence. The day was misty, with a hazy sun shining faintly. On our left was the moor we'd crossed and on our right the land sloped steeply upwards, hiding the castle. And the dragon.

"We ought to keep an eye out for Gethin's man," said Oz.

But the open moorland looked empty, as far as you could see through the haze. My mind was all on the monster waiting for us. At last the hillside veered to the right and lowered a little. We stopped. There was the gap ahead, waiting for us, the break in the hills leading into the valley.

"Now you two must stay out of sight," said Bronwen. "We'll have to find somewhere where you can see me but not be seen, if we can."

We could hear the dragon's breathing, that deep, regular rumbling sound. Oz wasn't looking so cheerful now and my stomach was turning over. Suddenly I grabbed hold of Bronwen's hands and held them tight.

"Thank you," I breathed. "If you really must do this, be so, so careful. And thank you!"

She squeezed my hands back and smiled at me. Then she pulled away and crept to the edge of the opening. Oz and me just stood there until she turned and beckoned us, at the same time putting a finger to her lips. We crept up and peered around the edge. And then my entire insides somersaulted.

I'd forgotten, I'd just forgotten, how terrifying she was. Her huge scaly head was resting on one of her front feet and little puffs of smoke blew out of her nostrils in time with her breathing. On either side of her mouth a lower tooth jutted out over her upper lip. They were massive, those fangs. They must have been a good three feet long. And her claws were not much shorter. In the hazy light her scales looked a dull bronze. Something moved and I realized it was the spiked tip of her tail, flicking as if to get rid of an irritating fly.

That's what we'd be to this creature – irritating flies. I really didn't want Bron to do this. We could just creep away now and the dragon probably wouldn't know we'd been here. But then, what about the runes? What about the promise I'd made to Woden? He never said it would be easy. But it was one thing to put myself in danger, and even Oz. But Bronwen?

Then she whispered to us. "Stay here. When I call you, come and bow low to her."

"But surely it'll be dangerous to wake her up," I whispered back.

Bronwen shrugged. "I'll do it very gently. I'll sing to her."

What?

But before I could stop her she'd walked up to the dragon and was standing about six feet away. Then she started a low, gentle singing, something like a lullaby.

Oz and me held our breath but nothing happened for a while. She went on singing this soothing song and suddenly one yellow eye opened. Bronwen sank to the ground in a low curtsey. The black slit in the eye moved around surveying the scene and I froze. Were we well enough hidden? Would the dragon recognize us? But her gaze moved back to Bron. The dragon lifted her head slightly. And then she spoke.

A shiver ran down my spine when I heard the dragon's voice. It was as if it came from the earth itself. A deep, deep voice, harsh and grating, like two swords scraping against each other. A whispering, creaking voice, not the roar we'd heard before. You could hear the crackle of fire in her belly, low now but ready to roar out her deadly flames.

Bron listened to it, then stood up and once more began her song. *The dragon liked her singing and seemed to have asked her to sing again*! Bronwen's sweet voice lifted to the hills, louder this time, more confident, and the dragon watched and listened. When Bron had finished, the dragon spoke again, as if asking a question, and Bronwen replied. I really wished I could speak Welsh. The conversation went on a little while, at one point Bron speaking for quite a time, as if she was explaining something. Then the dragon lifted her head and sat with her two front legs supporting it. She said something briefly and Bron turned to us and beckoned.

Oh my God! I felt as if I was walking to the gallows and I could tell by Oz's face that he felt the same. As soon as we reached Bron we practically fell face down in front of the monster. It was a relief not to look at her but I was still expecting a blast of fire to finish me off. There was a horrible silence and then she said something which Bron translated to us.

"She wants to know if you're both really sorry for sneaking up on her from the back."

"Oh yes, yes! We're really sorry!" I said, and at the same time Oz said, "Yeah, we'll never ever do it again!"

"We didn't know!" I pleaded.

"Yeah!" said Oz. "We had no idea!"

Both our noses were still pressed into the ground as neither of us had the guts to look up.

The dragon spoke again and I almost, *almost*, thought I heard a quiver of amusement in its voice.

"She wants you to stand up and look at her," said Bron.

We stood up, though it was hard to look into those long golden eyes with their jet-black slits. She spoke again, quite a long speech this time.

"She says you may go into the castle on condition that I go with you. But as soon as you have found these things that you are looking for you must go away from here and leave her in peace."

"Oh thank you, thank you," I said.

"And we'll never, ever bother you again," said Oz.

Judging by the expression on his face I knew Oz was feeling the same as me, that the very last thing either of us wanted to do was bother this monster again. Or go within a hundred miles of it, come to that.

The dragon lifted her head to the sky and made a little, "Puh!" sound, which sent a few small jets of flame into the air. I jumped. What did that mean? Then she started to uncoil herself, her head going one way and her tail slithering in the opposite direction.

A gap appeared where the dragon's head had been. A gate of wood and iron, already open. And beyond that yawned, pitch black, the entrance to Gethin's castle.

CHAPTER EIGHTEEN

This was it. The end of our quest, the charge that Woden had laid on me. I could hardly believe that all we had to do now was walk into the castle and find the runes. And give them back to Woden. He hadn't exactly been clear about how we were going to do that, but I was sure he'd show us. But first, of course, we had to walk past the dragon.

"Bow to her!" whispered Bron urgently, so we bowed down low and once again muttered our thanks.

Then we stood up and made our way past the dragon's head and through the gate. I kept my eyes on the shadowy doorway into the castle, which wasn't very welcoming but at least meant I didn't have to look into those golden eyes with their cat-like black slits. They gazed down at us, impossible to read. Who knew what kind of thoughts a dragon has in its head. Bronwen said something in Welsh and dropped another deep curtsey. The dragon said nothing, but slightly dipped her great head.

And then we were in, past the dragon, past the gate, past the archway of the door, and in the dim light of a stone corridor.

"Phew," breathed Oz. "Made it! Where now?"

"Down," I replied. "Gethin's dungeon was right at the bottom."

"Get your flint out," he said. "We'll have to light Bron's candle in a minute."

There were arrow slits in the walls, letting in enough light until we went underground. But we didn't seem to be *going* underground. We took the downward sloping path and soon reached some steps heading down into the bowels of the castle. They were treacherous, partly crumbled away, and we all held on to the wall to steady ourselves. By now it should have been pitch black, but the arrow slits were still there, still letting in shafts of murky light. Then the corridor came to an abrupt end. A great wooden door barred the way, but there was a key in the lock, a massive ornate iron key.

"This isn't right," I said. "Why aren't we underground yet? We've been going down for a while."

"And what's on the other side of that door?" said Oz.

"Well, let's find out, shall we?" said Bronwen brightly, so I took hold of the key.

It turned easily enough, though the creaking noise would have told the whole castle someone was turning it. We looked at each other, I took a deep breath and gingerly pushed at the door. It swung open and we blinked. Light flooded into the dim corridor. Ordinary daylight.

Oz pushed past me and stepped through.

"What the…?" he gasped, as I followed with Bronwen.

We were up on the battlements. The watery sun was still shining and a light wind was clearing the mist so we could see for miles through the gap in the hills. The breeze ruffled my hair as I walked to the edge and peered over. There was the dragon, now snoozing again below us.

"How did that happen?" I shook my head. "We *were* going down, weren't we? It wasn't my imagination, was it? How did we get up here?"

"Magic," said Bronwen. "This isn't going to be easy."

I walked along the battlements, gazing at the hilltops surrounding the castle and then at the distant view of moorland through the pass. I was baffled. But what Bron said made sense.

All right, then. Ordinary rules didn't apply in this place.

"So if going down led us up to the top," I said, "perhaps we should try going up and see if that leads us down."

Oz folded his arms.

"Got a ladder?" he smirked. "Or perhaps we should try growing some wings."

"Well obviously not from here," I snapped. "But if we go back inside and retrace our steps a bit, there might be some steps leading upwards. Got any better ideas?"

"No, let's try that," said Bronwen. "Come on then."

And she headed back through the door.

The steps were now going downwards, as you would expect, but they started to wind round, as if we were in a tower.

"This is mad," muttered Oz.

The light faded and soon we reached the last arrow slit. It seemed we might be heading in the right direction after all. We stopped on the crumbling steps while I got out my flint and firesteel, all the more precious now that the dragon had burnt Oz's to a cinder.

Or had it? A thought flashed through my head as I kept striking the flint and steel together. Oz's fire gear might well have been the only things in his bag to survive the dragon's fiery blast, but we hadn't gone back to look. We'd had too many other things on our minds. Like staying alive.

Bron patiently held her candle at the ready while I fumbled around for what seemed like an age.

"Come on, come on," I muttered. "Light, you stupid thing."

The air was damp and chill, but at last I got a spark. The touchwood started to smoulder and soon the candle was flaring into life. It was a welcome homely presence in the gloom. I spat on the touchwood and squashed the embers between my fingers before putting it all back in my bag. Finally we could carry on down.

Then our stairway met another, going up.

"What do we do?" said Oz.

"I think we do what Wulf suggested," said Bronwen. "Go up and hope it leads us down."

I was expecting Oz to argue, but he just shrugged. So we climbed the second stairway and it didn't lead us to arrowslits and daylight. Perhaps this time we were really were heading down to Gethin's dungeon.

After a while we reached a sort of landing with wooden doors off it. Some of them were half hanging off their hinges.

"Cells," said Oz. "I was in one of these." He looked around. "I can't remember which one."

Bronwen held the candle up so we could see better.

"This place is enormous," she said. "I've never seen anything like it. It's nothing like Lord Aelfric's hall, or even the hall of that other magician,

Grimwold, though his place was grand enough. But all this stone. All these different levels. It's amazing."

"It's been a bit knocked about since I was here before," I said. "Probably in the time change."

"Do you know what I'm thinking?" shuddered Bronwen. "Especially after this going up, going down stuff. I think this whole castle was built by magic. It has an eerie feel about it. I *really* don't want to spend too long here."

"So let's get moving," said Oz. "The sooner we're out of here the better."

There was a narrow flight of steps on the other side of the landing, leading on up to who knew where. Mad as it sounds, I thought it might lead to the dungeon at the very bottom of the castle. We stayed close together, me in front, then Bron holding her candle and last of all Oz, who kept looking back to check we weren't being followed. The walls felt cold and damp to our touch and the steps were slippery, so our going was slow. After a while the stairway widened out but we kept to one side so we could hold on to the wall. Then it stopped.

Bron held up the candle. We were in a chamber of some kind, or a hall. I realized that the walls were now solid rock, as if we were at last deep underground. The chamber led to somewhere else because facing us was another one of those enormous wooden doors. This might well be it, but now we'd arrived my courage was failing me. If the castle was still full of Gethin's magic, what was on the other side of the door?

I think we were all feeling the same because we just stood staring at it. A great, heavy, oaken thing with a carving of something in the middle. Then...were my eyes going funny? The carving seemed to shimmer. Wisps of mist flowed out of it and began to form a shape. A man shape, which grew in height. We stepped back. Bron gave a little squeak, but kept hold of the candle.

The shape grew yet taller and more solid and then...what I was dreading most of all...

From the top of its head sprouted a pair of enormous antlers.

CHAPTER NINETEEN

I shrank back. We all did. I wanted to run but my feet wouldn't move. The figure grew more and more solid and details started to appear. It was dressed in black, though I wasn't looking at its clothes. I couldn't take my eyes off Gethin's face, at first indistinct then clearer and clearer. His piercing dark eyes bored into mine as the white bone headdress, the deer's skull with its branching antlers, began to glow in the shadows.

Suddenly a voice cried out, "Begone, foul spirit!" and we were plunged into blackness.

"What?!" shrieked Oz, and I started laughing.

I was a bit hysterical, I admit, but also…I knew what had happened.

"Well done, Bron," I said. "Though it's a shame the candle had to go out."

"Well, *you* try throwing a candle at an apparition without it going out," replied Bronwen.

Then Oz started laughing as well, in the same shaky hysterical way as me.

"Got to admit it, Bron," he said. "It's a good job the person with the candle was the one who kept a cool head."

"Why, thank you, Osric," she answered. "My nain told me about things like this. Sendings, she called them. They frighten you half to death, but that's the only real harm they can do you."

"Well done, Bron," I said. "Now all we've got to do is find the candle and relight it."

But I wasn't as confident as I sounded. Even as I crouched down to look for the candle my eyes were still trained on the spot where Gethin's face had appeared. There was nothing to see of course. We were in pitch black.

We groped around the cold stone floor, and then Oz yelled again.

"What's the matter?" I hissed.

"Sorry," he laughed in the same shaky way. "Must have been a spider. It ran over my hand."

"Sh!" whispered Bronwen. "What's that?"

Then I heard it too. A scuttling noise to my right. Then another to my left. And then another behind.

"Oh, Diew," gasped Bronwen. "I hope they're mice and not rats. I hate rats!"

I didn't much like the idea of feeling around and putting my hand on a rat. Or being bitten by one. But gradually the scuttling died away and almost at the same moment me and Oz called out, "Got it!"

My hand had closed round the comforting smooth feel of a candle and Oz had found it too. But when we lifted it up it didn't feel right. Bronwen had thrown it so hard against the door that it had broken in two.

"This is no good," said Oz. "I'll cut it in half. It's big enough to make a pair of candles."

I could hear him slide his knife out of his boot. Then he carefully found the bit of wick that was the only thing keeping the two halves together and sliced it through.

"I've got the top end, I think," I said, still keeping my eyes on where the door was, even though I couldn't see it.

Light! I was desperate for a bit of light! I rummaged in my bag, got out my flint and steel and once again struggled, in the deep blackness, to light my bit of candle. I got Bron to hold it and never have I been more pleased to see the flicker of homely yellow light.

Then Oz whittled away at the tallow of his end. When he'd freed some wick we lit that from the candle flame. Luckily it had been a big candle and a clean break, so now we had two sources of light.

I took a deep breath. "We mustn't let these go out," I said. "And we've got to be prepared for more stuff like that thing on the other side of the door. Can you get rid of these...what did you call them?"

"Sendings," prompted Bron.

"Right. Can we get rid of them without actually throwing the candle and breaking it into even smaller bits?"

"Yes, I'm sorry about that. I think I should have just thrust the flame into it, but I sort of panicked. I wasn't even quite sure it *was* a sending."

"No, you did brilliantly, Bron," I reassured her. "I'd probably have just dropped the candle."

"Yeah, well never mind all that," said Oz. "Let's get on with it."

I couldn't see a handle so we pushed at the door. And shoved. And stood back and threw ourselves at it. We did that for ages. It didn't budge.

"Oh, I hope it doesn't need a spell," said Bronwen, "or we'll never do it."

"Did your nain teach you any words for opening doors?" I panted, while Oz carried on straining and grunting.

"No, we didn't do that sort of magic," she shook her head.

"Let's sit down," I said. "I need to get my breath."

Bronwen and I sat on the floor, holding a candle each, but Oz didn't want to give up. He leaned on the door and when his breathing was even he started to feel it all over.

"Hang on, what's this?" he said.

His hand was on the carving in the middle. The thing that Gethin's apparition had floated out of.

"Feel this," he said, and I put my hand where his had been.

There was a tiny piece of metal, a little catch, and as I touched it the door slowly swung open. Slowly, slowly, creak, creak, it opened on to darkness. A foul smell wafted out to us and we doubled up coughing and put our hands in front of our mouths and noses.

"It smells like a graveyard," I choked out.

"One where they forgot to bury the bodies," coughed Oz.

"Wait, have some water," gasped Bronwen.

She pulled a leather water bottle out of her bag and we each took a gulp, grateful for the clean, wholesome taste.

"We'll get used to it in a minute," gasped Bron.

"I think it's getting less," I said. "That door's been shut a long time and now we've let some air in it won't be so bad."

"But what made the smell?" said Oz with a funny expression on his face.

"Just magic," I shrugged.

"No, not *just* magic," he said. "I've got an idea where it might come from. Look at that light."

We stepped to the doorway and saw a sickly glow where there had been pitch black. A wavering, greenish glow in the middle of the cellar, with some indistinct shape in the middle.

"A corpse light," whispered Oz.

In the candlelight his face looked the same colour as the sickly green of...whatever it was.

All three of us moved just inside the doorway and peered at the light and the thing in its centre.

And then we saw what it was.

CHAPTER TWENTY

Something was hanging from a rope. Something in an old green shirt that Oz used to wear. Its head was at a funny angle, a head with straw coloured hair like Oz's. Slowly it swung round and I was prepared for the bulging eyes and distorted features of a hanged boy. But I wasn't prepared for what I saw.

The face was rotting away, half skull and half putrid flesh. And out of one eye socket wriggled a fat white maggot.

Bronwen gasped and hid her face, while Oz rushed back through the door. I could hear him retching outside. My stomach heaved but I forced myself to remember that it wasn't real. Was it?

I gripped my candle and tried to get the courage to go up to it. But then an invisible hand cut the rope and the thing fell on the ground with a flump. *So it wasn't just some ghostly apparition! It made a noise as it fell*!

I watched, frozen in horror, as it started to twitch, to jerk around and try to stand up. Bronwen clutched my arm and I pulled her closer to me. But neither of us moved any closer to the *thing*.

In a series of spasms it managed to get to its feet, though it wobbled unsteadily. The head started to jerk around as if the sightless eyes were looking for something. They seemed to fix on us and Bron gave a little moan. I thought the horror was complete, but then its jaw moved as if it were trying to speak.

At that point Oz rushed back, grabbed my candle and ran at it. He thrust the flame deep into the creature's middle and, with a sigh which echoed round the cavern, it crumpled to the floor and faded away.

Oz stood there, panting, then he too crumpled up on to the floor.

"And may your soul rest in peace," he sobbed.

I just stood there, while Oz tried to control his heaving shoulders.

When he'd calmed down a bit I said, "It was him, wasn't it, that boy that Gethin hanged."

He nodded.

"But it wasn't like the first sending," I went on. "It was more solid. It made a noise when it hit the floor."

"He set these things up," said Bron. "Gethin, I mean, so that anyone who came here would be scared off. He must have done it before the rune ceremony that turned back time."

"But in that case," I said, "I don't understand how he did this one. I mean, he'd only just hanged the boy when I was brought in. Would he have had time to turn this into a sending?"

"And very clever, too, to make it seem as if the body had been there a long time."

"Shut up!" said Oz. "Just shut up! I don't care how he did it. I just want to get the runes and get out of here."

"You're right," I said. "Let's just find the things."

I wanted to find them and get out myself, but also I knew it was best for Oz. He'd seen the boy hang and this had brought it all back to him. Looking for the runes would give him something else to think about.

And it seemed our luck was finally in.

"Look!" said Bronwen. "What's that pile of old stones over there?"

It was them, over by the cavern wall! A pile of ancient looking rune-stones!

Or was it another sending? Another one of Gethin's tricks?

We ran over and I reached out and touched them, hesitantly, holding one in my hand and feeling its weight and worn surface.

"I think it's them." I couldn't help grinning. Then I started to space them out on the floor, looking to see if they were all there.

"Can I see yours again?" asked Bron.

So I drew it out from under my shirt and showed her.

"Yes, they're the same!" she said. "And there's yours! Oh, but…how can it be here in the pile and round your neck at the same time?"

"Something to do with the time shift," I said. "I'd given it to Gethin. I had to, or else he'd have started cutting little bits off Oz. But then when time went backwards a bit, I'd still have got mine round my neck…I think."

"They're not all old," frowned Oz. "A few of them look newer, more like your mum's."

"No, that's right," I said. "I'd forgotten. Gethin didn't have a complete set of the original ones." I paused, thinking. "Oh well, we'll just have to give this lot to Woden and he can sort it out."

"What a weird place this is," said Bron, standing up. She held up her candle and started to walk round the cavern. Animal skulls gazed down on us from the walls. She shuddered. "Put the runes in your bag and let's go."

Then she tripped over something and lowered the candle to see what it was.

"Oh, no," she gasped, and me and Oz stopped picking up the stones and looked.

Oz let out a long sigh. "I thought this was suddenly getting a bit easy," he said.

For by the light of the candle we saw another pile of rune-stones.

My brain seemed to have slowed down and I said the most obvious thing.

"So…how will we know which are the real ones?"

"Well, let's have a really good look," said Bron in her matter-of-fact way.

But the really good look showed them to be absolutely identical.

"We'll just have to put them all in the bag and let your Woden sort it out," she went on, and I loved her for being so sensible.

Oz gave a hollow laugh. "We're gonna need a big bag," he snorted. "Look at this."

He started walking round the walls holding up a candle. Under each animal skull was a pile of rune-stones. Old, worn rune-stones, each pile the same as all the others. Heaps and heaps of ancient rune-stones. When he got to a curtain – the one he'd been kept behind at the beginning of Gethin's ceremony – he pulled it back.

Higher than Oz himself towered a pile of stones with runes etched into them, all looking worn and older than time itself.

"We'd need a dozen chests to shovel this lot into," he said. "And a couple of horse-drawn carts to carry them away."

None of us said anything. Then my bewilderment suddenly turned to anger.

"All right, Woden!" I shouted. "What do we do now?"

CHAPTER TWENTY-ONE

My voice echoed round and round the cellar, loud at first, then fainter and fainter till it faded away.

And what happened then? Did Huginn and Muninn flap in to help us sort out the stones. No.

Did Sleipnir, Woden's eight-legged horse, gallop in to carry the right stones back to his master? No.

Did Woden himself appear and say, "Well done. Thank you. I'll take over from here."? You must be joking.

But something *did* happen. He likes to make you work, does Woden, the rune master. He likes to make you use your brains.

The rune-stone on its leather thong round my neck startled to tingle. It warmed up, until it got so hot it almost burned me. And my mind was flooded with pictures of all the times it had helped me, all the times it had protected me. And I realized that I'd been ignoring it, treating it as if it were just an ornament, a piece of jewellery. What a fool I'd been.

I hadn't got my memories back when we were fighting in the army, so I couldn't remember then what the rune-stone could do. But once Woden and the ravens had shown me all those amazing adventures we'd had… once I knew what powers the stone had…then there'd been times when I *could* have used it, asked it for protection. But I hadn't thought of it. And now it wanted to tell me something.

"Ow!" I yelled. "Stop doing that, it hurts!"

"What!?" said Oz and Bronwen at the same time.

Oz jumped to his feet, dagger at the ready, while Bron stood there looking alarmed.

"Stop burning me!" I almost laughed as I held the stone away from my skin.

"Look!" exclaimed Bron. "It's glowing!"

I slipped the thong over my head and held it up, so that the stone dangled in mid-air. It shone with a golden light as it swung to and fro, and I could feel the warmth even when it wasn't next to my skin.

Then my eye was caught by another light some feet away. In one of the piles by the wall, like the last glowing ember in a fire, shone another little rune-stone. All the others in the pile were lifeless but this one twinkled back at mine as if they were sending messages to each other.

I skidded across to it on my knees and pulled it out, blowing on my fingers as I did so. This one too was burning hot. It was Gyfu, gift, and I set it on the ground with my Thorn rune next to it.

"It's all right!" I grinned. "All the real ones will be glowing like these. All we've got to do is find them." Then, as an afterthought, "Um, thanks, Woden."

"Here's another one!" called Bronwen, burrowing into another little mound where you could just see the glint of the half-buried stone.

"And another!" shouted Oz, and now we were all scrabbling round in the piles of rune-stones around the walls.

"But what about this lot?" said Bron, standing by the huge heap behind the curtain.

"That's easy!" said Oz. He stood up and gave the pile of stones a massive kick, laughing as they flew all over the place.

It was good to see him enjoying himself and I was tempted to join in. But I didn't.

"Come on, Oz," I grinned. "Better get a move on."

I put my own rune-stone back round my neck but outside my shirt – it was still a bit hot – and started to get organized.

We spread them out and sifted through until we had eighteen rune-stones in all. Then we laid those on the ground where they twinkled like jewels or like glow-worms in the night. So as well as the light from the two candles in that dark cavernous dungeon, we had a little line of glowing stones. They shone even brighter when the candlelight wasn't on them.

"How many of the originals did Gethin have?" asked Bronwen.

I shrugged. "That's the trouble. I don't know. But there were a fair number of gaps that he'd filled in with new ones."

"And how many *should* there be in all?" she went on.

"Twenty-four," said Oz without hesitation. "I'm looking to see which ones are missing. "There's Sigil and Mann, Ethel and Lagu."

I looked at Oz as he went muttering through, naming the runes as if he'd been doing it all his life. He really knew his stuff.

"There's Eh, the horse rune," I said. "He must have got that from you, Oz. D'you remember, you took it from the body of Grimwold's man?"

"Yeah, course I remember. And you were there too, Bron – at Brother Walter's place?"

She nodded.

"And then Gethin took it off me," Oz went on.

"Do you know what?" said Bronwen. "We haven't really got time for reminiscing. Let's put these in the bag and have one more check that we haven't missed any. And then let's go."

She was right, of course. She always was. So we walked all round the cellar spreading the stones out with our feet, checking and double checking that we hadn't left any of the precious little glow-worms undiscovered.

"Right," said Oz, starting to pick them up. "Into the bag they go and away *we* go."

We all crouched as Oz put them in the leather bag, pulling the cord and shutting in their light. Bron was holding one candle and I had the other, now the only two sources of light in the cellar.

Or were they? Suddenly a cold white light shone above us. We all looked up and then scrambled backwards.

The stag's skull above us had started to give out a ghostly glow. Then its eyes gleamed red and it started to move. The skull dipped, and turned from side to side as if stretching after a sleep. A little below it something else appeared in the wall. Something white, shifting around as if stuck. A wriggle, and it was through – the stag's bony front leg. The hoof started to paw the ground with a rattling sound.

We were backing towards the door by now, and when the leg was followed by a second leg, and then the whole spectral skeleton began to ease itself into the dungeon, we didn't wait to see any more.

All three of us turned and fled.

CHAPTER TWENTY-TWO

We ran. We didn't know which way we were going, we just wanted to get away. But it was only a sending! Why hadn't we tried to get rid of it with the candle flame? I can only say that some terror had gripped us all, sending us slightly mad. We couldn't think straight. We just ran.

And after us galloped the skeleton, its hooves clopping and rattling on the ground. We ran upstairs and downstairs, along dark corridors, not having a clue which way we were going. The candle flames wavered as we ran, briefly illuminating the rough stone walls and then plunging them into darkness again behind us. The stag didn't speed up, it just kept the same steady pace as us.

I simply didn't have the guts to stop and thrust the candle at it and I didn't want to throw it and lose one of our two sources of light. If the other candle blew out we'd have been in complete blackness. But something was nagging at my mind. Something I'd been thinking very recently but I couldn't remember what it was. Then when yet another flight of steps confronted us it came to me.

We raced up as fast as we could, though we were getting breathless, and at the top I stopped and turned round.

"What are you doing?" gasped Oz.

The skeleton stopped at the foot of the steps and looked up at us with its glowing red eyes. Then it put one hoof on the bottom step.

I held up my rune-stone and with as much voice as I could muster I said, "By the power of Thorn I command you to stop!"

The stag threw back its head and made a weird kind of baying noise. Then it shook itself so that all it bones rattled, and carried on up the steps towards us.

The rune-stone didn't work!

"Run!" I yelled, and we carried on with our panic-stricken flight.

Why hadn't it worked? Had the stone lost its power or did it only work on living creatures? My mind blanked out as we careered down yet another flight of steps. There was a door at the bottom. Oh, please let it open or we'd be trapped!

Oz reached it first and flung himself at it. It creaked open so easily that he fell through...on to the battlements! Daylight flooded in and me and Bron panted out after Oz, who was already racing across to the other side of the walkway round the top of the castle.

But there were no other doors. We were still trapped.

"If he comes round one way, we'll go the other," gasped Oz.

"Oh, no," moaned Bronwen. "I'm not going in there again."

We stood looking at the skeleton, which was standing in the doorway pawing the ground.

"It's wondering which way to come at us," muttered Oz.

"We really should try that candle thing," I panted.

"What, go right up to it?" said Bron. "Have you got the courage?"

"No," I answered. "What about you, Oz?"

Then a ray of sun came from behind a cloud and shone into the doorway. The stag backed away, making that weird baying sound.

"Oh, thank you, Diew!" said Bronwen. "It doesn't like the sunlight, or even the daylight, I think."

"Yeah, that's really great," said Oz. "So we sit and wait till it gets dark and it trots out and gets us."

"What about climbing down?" I suggested, peering over the parapet.

It looked a very long way down. A very long way, with not much in the way of footholds. And at the bottom...the red gold scales of the dragon gleamed in the late afternoon sun. I could imagine what that dragon would do if we jumped on to her and woke her from her doze. The other two looked over as well, and then Bronwen started laughing.

"It's all right, Bron, don't get hysterical," I said. "We'll think of something."

"I'm not hysterical!" she went on laughing. "We're saved! Don't you see?"

Me and Oz looked at each other. We didn't see.

Bronwen leaned over and called, "Tanllyd! Oh, Tanllyd!"

There was a noise like bits of metal being rubbed together and then, over the top of the wall appeared a spiky neck, which unfurled to reveal an enormous bronze head. Slowly, slowly it came into view and not so slowly Oz and I shrank back. The great golden eyes took in everything…us, the walkway and the door to the corridor, with the skeletal stag hovering a little way inside. The dragon gazed at the stag and then threw back her head. A spurt of flame shot into the sky.

"Oh, Tanllyd, please help us!" begged Bron, and then remembered herself. She dropped a deep curtsey and the rest of the conversation was in Welsh. I say conversation because the dragon had a great deal to say as well as Bronwen. That voice! It was a shock, though we'd heard it before. It whispered and creaked – a deep, deep voice, ancient yet still full of power.

I was just beginning to wonder when the talking was going to stop, all the while keeping an eye on the stag in case it decided it didn't mind the sunlight after all, when Bronwen turned to us.

"Tanllyd has very, very kindly agreed to lower us to the ground. It's really good of her, so please bow."

We both bowed low, but I could see by the expression on Oz's face that he was thinking the same as me. How on earth was this going to work?

"Thank you," said Bronwen crisply. "She'll allow us to climb on to her neck and hold on to her spikes while she lowers us. But probably not all three together."

What?

"But she's not all that happy about you boys, so she wants me to go with one of you, then she'll lift me up again and take the other one."

"Why can't we all go together?" objected Oz.

"Don't argue!" said Bronwen. "She's saving our lives here, so just do what she says…And you can bow again."

We bowed again.

"You first," said Oz.

"No, please, after you," I muttered.

"Oh, stop messing around!" snapped Bronwen. "She'll change her mind if you carry on like this. Osric, come here!"

Oz did as he was told, but the smirk was wiped off my face when I glanced back and saw the skeleton watching us intently. The dragon yawned, giving us a terrifying view of her teeth, then she turned her head away and angled her neck so that it was right by the parapet wall.

"See, we should be able to fit in between these two spikes," said Bron.

She clambered up on to the wall and carefully shifted herself on to the dragon's neck, holding on to one of its spikes. That girl had some courage.

"Now you," she said to Oz. "Get on behind me and put your arms round my waist."

Oz looked much less cool about the whole thing than Bronwen, but he managed, and once he was on, Bron said something to the dragon.

I was expecting the dragon to lower them gently to the ground, but the head and neck swung away up into the air before swooping down.

"Whoa!" shouted Oz.

I leaned over and watched him jump off. Just then a massive black cloud scudded across the weak sun and we were plunged into gloom. A rattling sound made me turn round. The stag was edging its way out of the door.

"Hurry up, Bron!" I yelled. "I think our friend's coming!"

What were they doing? I could hear talking down below. The stag took a few tentative steps on to the battlement.

"Get a move on!" I shouted. "The thing's coming for me! I'll have to jump!"

I never thought I'd be so pleased to see the ugly great head of a dragon rearing up beside me. As soon as I saw Bron I tried to scramble on. But it wasn't quite in position and I nearly fell through the gap between its neck and the wall. Desperately I grabbed at a spike, and dangled there with my feet waving madly.

Then the dragon pushed her neck right up against the wall, crushing me between hot dragon scales and cold castle stones. I think she was trying to help but she nearly squashed all the air out of me. Bron said something to her, and as she shifted away from the wall she hauled me up. Somehow I found myself sitting between Bronwen in front and another spike at my back. It seemed as if that dragon knew what she was doing, as the space between two spikes was just right for two people, but if you'd been sitting there on your own you'd have been sliding around all over the place. But would a dragon think of that? Probably not. Once I'd got my breath back she was even sort of comfortable and pleasantly hot. I imagined the fire crackling away in the creature's belly.

"Hang on to me!" said Bron, as if I was going to do anything else.

Then the sun came out again and my last sight of the stag was of it clattering back into its dark doorway.

"Ha! Thought you'd got me!" I yelled at it as we swung away, up into the air and down to the ground.

Forget comfortable. I slid off feeling as if I'd left my stomach somewhere up in the sky.

After that there was a lot more bowing and curtseying and more conversation between Bronwen and the dragon. Finally she went up and raised her arms while the dragon dipped its great head. And to my amazement she kissed its nose.

"I'm gonna call you Dragon Girl," said Oz as we walked away.

He was obviously impressed. So was I.

We'd got the runes and we'd escaped, but all I wanted to do now was curl up and go to sleep. Preferably after a hearty meal.

"I can't believe we were only in there for one day," said Oz as we trudged back to Bron's hut in the forest.

"No, it seems like a week," agreed Bronwen. "And what do we now? How do we get the runes back to your Woden?"

"No idea," I said. "We'll think about that tomorrow. Have you got any of that stew left?"

"Yes," said Bron. "Don't worry."

And then there was no more talking till we reached the edge of the forest. We were all too bone weary to do anything but put one foot in front of the other. The trees seemed welcoming, because we knew we were nearly there.

They seemed welcoming, that is, until a group of men stepped out from behind them, swords drawn and mocking smiles on their faces. Their leader walked towards us. He had pale skin, high cheekbones and shoulder-length dark hair.

It was him.

Gethin's man.

The one we'd met a few days ago. The one who wanted to use the runes to bring his master back from the dead.

"Ah, useful fools," he sneered. "You've saved me a lot of trouble." He held out his hand. "Now give me the runes."

CHAPTER TWENTY-THREE

There was no fight left in me. No energy to do anything at all or even to think straight. I just wanted to collapse at his feet and give him the runes.

So it was a good job that I didn't have them.

Oz did.

Though what could we do? I couldn't believe my friends would be feeling any better than I was.

But *my* rune-stone wasn't going to give up that easily. It started to warm up and tingle against my skin. It woke up my brain.

Of course! I could use it against this man! But there were so many of them, six as well as him. I'd also been thrown by the fact that Thorn hadn't worked against the skeleton stag. And by the time I'd said the words I'd probably have an arrow in me. I needed a distraction. And Oz provided one.

"What a shame we haven't got them," he said, cool as you like.

"Yes," said Bronwen. "We left them with the dragon. They're quite safe with her."

Oh blessed friends! They were doing much better than me.

"Of course," Oz went on, "she'd probably let you have them if you asked nicely. You speak Welsh, don't you?"

"Yes, she's very reasonable really," said Bron.

Gethin's man was looking quite irritated by now, but he wasn't looking at me. Carefully I drew Thorn out from under my shirt.

"You know that we could just kill you and take them, don't you?" he snapped.

"Ah, but isn't there something about them having to be given up willingly?" said Oz.

By the time he'd got to the end of his sentence I'd got to the end of mine, "*By the power of Thorn I command you to stop*!" and our enemy was lying pole-axed on the ground.

Oz whipped out his sword and leapt on one of the men. All six were so confused by what had happened that they couldn't decide whether to fight or try to avoid my rune. But that didn't last long. One of them was crouching by his master, listening to check if he was breathing, but the others were soon trying to overpower us.

It wasn't too difficult for them. Oz and his opponent clashed swords fiercely but he was soon trying to fend off two men, while I held up my rune and tried to stun another one. Someone leapt at me, knocking the rune-stone out of my hand. It swung free on its leather thong as I stumbled backwards. Somehow I unsheathed my own sword as the man shoved me hard into a tree trunk.

"Give us those runes, you little worm!" he growled.

I tried to swing my sword but I wasn't in a good position, so although I caught his arm I didn't do any damage. But I managed to knee him off me and parry his next sword thrust. He was stronger than me and I was worn out, but I was also younger and more agile than him. So when he swung his sword at my neck I easily ducked and dodged it. I caught a glimpse of Oz doing similar ducking and dodging and managing to trip one opponent up and send him sprawling. But then I was grabbed from behind and my arms were pinned to my sides.

Unable to move I suddenly thought of Bronwen. She had no weapon and no dragon to defend her.

"Run, Bron!" I shouted – too late.

One of them had her in an iron grip with his sword at her neck. I should have thought of her before, but there'd been no time! And what could I have done?

The brute opened his mouth to speak...but the words never came.

He fell back with an arrow in his throat.

Then another man was down with an arrow in his chest and I managed to whip Thorn out again and stun another one. Out of seven men, two were dead, two were knocked out by my rune-stone and the other three turned tail and fled. *We* were easy prey but invisible archers were too much for them. And then only two were fleeing, as another went down with an arrow in his back, while one arrow went slightly wide of its mark and landed in a tree.

What was happening here? Had Woden suddenly decided to give us a hand? Maybe, but he wasn't using supernatural means.

Two hooded figures ran up with scarves across their faces. Two human figures. Their bows were poised for another shot, but the men had gone. We heard horses neighing and the sound of galloping.

"Leave them," said the taller of the two.

"Pity," said the other, pulling off the hood and scarf. Corn coloured plaits fell out from under the hood and a girl grinned at us.

"Don't show your face so soon!" said our other saviour, obviously a boy.

"Oh, *they're* all right," said the girl. "How did you do that?" She pointed at the two men lying on the ground with no arrows in them.

The other one was already bending over them, looking for signs of injury.

"They're just stunned," I said, "but the trouble is it won't last long, so we'd better tie them up. And thank you!"

"Yeah, thanks," said Oz.

"We're really grateful," said Bronwen, "but I've got to say this." She took a deep breath. "That's the last time I'm going anywhere without my bow and arrow! And I'm thinking you can teach me to use a sword as well."

The girl laughed. "Good idea."

Then she looked at her companion, already trussing the two stunned men with rope from his bag.

"As you can see, my brother doesn't waste time."

"Don't kill them in cold blood!" said Bronwen. "They're not fighting any more."

"I wasn't going to," he said. "I wouldn't bother tying them up if I was going to slit their throats. Help me tie them to a couple of horses. I'll ride another and lead all of them away from here. With a bit of luck they'll be some miles away by the time they come to. I'll have to walk back, so tell Mum I'll help myself to supper when I get in."

He looked at us over the top of his scarf.

"I reckon you could do with food and some sleep. And then you can tell us exactly how you stunned them."

Food. Sleep. With those magic words in our ears we shoved the two living bodies on to two of the horses tethered nearby and bound them with rope.

"You'd better take these bodies too, Stig," said the girl. "We don't want them hanging round here unburied, with their ghosts coming back to haunt us."

"Good thinking, little sis," said Stig. "And a good job we've got a lot of rope!"

So we bound the dead bodies as well to the remaining horses, one on its own and two together, to leave a horse free for Stig. Then he moved around stroking their noses and whispering in their ears, though he still kept his hood up and his scarf over his face. I watched astonished as the horses nuzzled him back and stood waiting to be told what to do. It reminded me of something I'd seen before, but I couldn't think what.

"Come on my friends," he said mounting one of them. "We're going for a little gallop."

And off they cantered, while we watched with our mouths open.

"How did he get them to do what he wanted?" asked Oz.

"Stig has a way with animals," said the girl. "Unlike me. I tell a sheep to go one way and it goes the other." She turned to Bronwen. "You're the girl who lives in the old hermit's hut, aren't you?"

"Well yes," said Bron. "But I haven't seen you before."

"Oh, we're good at seeing without being seen."

"And you're English," said Oz. "I thought everyone round here was Welsh."

"Not at all," said the girl. "These are border lands."

"That's right," nodded Bron. "Not like where I was born. Everyone there was Welsh."

"What I was going to say was that you won't be able to stay there now. So do you want to collect a few things and we'll all go back to our place for tonight."

So that's what we did. Bron did indeed only have a few things to bring, and she said goodbye to the hut with some regret.

"But you may be able to come back after a while," said the girl. "I'm sorry, I haven't told you my name. I'm Hild, and you are?"

We introduced ourselves and started the long walk to her home. It wasn't only the thought of food and sleep that kept us going. Hild was an entertaining companion and cheerfully answered our questions.

"We're shepherds," she said. "We look after the flock that belonged to Lord Gethin, but two years ago he vanished, thank God, so the sheep more or less belong to us now. Anyway, until someone comes back and claims them. It was weird. It happened round about the time that the Normans came – though we only heard rumours of that, and so far they haven't bothered us much. About that time Lord Gethin just disappeared and we were *so* glad."

Of course, she had no idea what *we* knew of Gethin's disappearance and I was pleased she seemed so happy about it.

"I can't tell you how good life has been since he vanished," she went on. "And the castle sort of collapsed in on itself a bit, and everyone left. Then a few months ago that dragon flew in, so that's another good reason to steer clear of the place. I never thought I'd see a dragon! I thought they were only in stories!"

Listening to her chatting made our legs less weary and our hearts lighter. I noticed that Oz couldn't take his eyes off her smiling face.

"But you haven't told us," said Bron, getting to the main point, "how you came to rescue us."

"Ah, we keep an eye on things," replied Hild. "Particularly that Madoc."

"Madoc!" interrupted Bron. "Of course! That was the name on the letter that you boys were supposed to deliver! You remember, two years ago."

Hild raised her eyebrows, and Oz said, "Yeah, we'll tell you about that another time."

"All right," said Hild. "I'll keep you to that. Anyway Stig had seen Madoc around lately, so we thought something was up. If anyone's going to take our sheep away it's him. We'd been watching the area carefully, and when he turned up with his band of men we knew he meant no good. It's as simple as that. Any enemy of Madoc's is our friend. And here we are at home!"

We'd been so absorbed in her story that we hadn't even noticed the little homestead. It was the usual small shepherd's cottage, made of wattle and daub. Even so it was a lot bigger than Bron's hut, and there was a cheerful curl of smoke wafting from the hole in the roof. Evening had drawn on but when Hild flung open the door we left the shadows outside and entered a room full of firelight and the wonderful smells of cooking. A black and white puppy jumped up at Hild and she laughed and ruffled its fur.

"We found some waifs and strays, Mum," said Hild, pushing the dog away and hugging her plump mother.

"Well, it's a good job there's plenty of stew, then," she smiled. "You can tell me your story when you've eaten. Where's Stig?"

"He'll be a while," said Hild. "He had to take some horses away and then he'll be walking back. Long story, tell you later. I'm starving!"

"Bring some more stools from the barn, Hild, and then you can sit yourselves down."

"I'll help," said Oz quickly.

And in no time at all we were holding bowls of steaming food, dished out by Hild's mother Edith. It was a feast. We were in heaven. Rich herby mutton stew with carrots, turnips, onions and – did I mention the mutton? But best of all was good fresh bread to soak up the juices. It seemed years since we'd had bread like that. The dog looked beseechingly at each of us in turn, until Hild threw it a mouthful.

We were too busy eating to talk, though Oz couldn't resist saying, "Are you sure it isn't Friday, Bron? Should you be eating meat?"

"Very funny, Osric. It was Friday yesterday, you dolt."

She rolled her eyes and carried on eating.

The meal had been mostly cleared away and we were discussing where everyone was going to sleep when the puppy started to bark joyfully. It wagged its tail like mad and threw itself at the door.

Stig walked in with a broad smile on his face and greeted his fluffy friend with almost as much enthusiasm as the dog showed. Then he smiled around at the rest of us. His scarf was gone and no hood covered his blonde hair.

Oz turned pale and staggered back as if he'd seen a ghost, knocking his stool over and clutching at my shoulder to steady himself.

"You're alive!" he gasped.

CHAPTER TWENTY-FOUR

Stig looked puzzled, then grinned again.

"Well, yes. It would seem they didn't kill me. I tied them up pretty well, you know. The two you stunned were awake by the time I left them." He laughed. "They were wriggling around and glaring at me, but my knots hold well."

Thank God – he thought Oz had been worried he'd be attacked!

"I hope you kept your mask on!" said his mother.

"Of course – especially as one of them was Madoc! I'm not daft, but I am hungry."

His mother hugged him and started to dish out some stew.

But I knew what Oz had meant. I knew why he thought for a moment he was seeing a ghost. We looked at each other and he tried to pull himself together but he was obviously still in shock. I was relieved Stig didn't ask any questions. How could we explain the truth to him?

Because Stig was the boy Gethin had hanged.

Just a few hours before, we'd seen his rotting corpse in Gethin's dungeon. I wasn't sure if Bronwen realized this, because the face on the sending had been so disfigured. But she could tell something strange was going on.

"Now we were just talking about where you're all going to sleep," said Edith, as if nothing had happened. She'd given Oz a shrewd look though, and I guessed she knew there was a story behind his behaviour.

"Your outhouse would be good," said Oz, "where we got the stools from. There's plenty of straw there."

She nodded. "And you, my dear," she said to Bron, "can stay in here with Hild and myself if you like. You'll be out with the sheep, Stig, won't you?"

Stig nodded, his mouth full of stew.

"Oh…I…thank you so much," said Bron, awkwardly. "It's very kind of you…all this is so kind of you…but we have something to discuss, Wulf and Oz and myself. I'd be very happy to sleep in the barn with them. It may not seem proper, but we're old friends and we're used to it."

"Oh, we're not bothered about proper, are we Mum?" said Hild.

"No, dear, if that's what you want," smiled Edith. "I can see you do have a lot to talk about, one way and another. I don't want to be nosy, but if you feel like sharing anything in the morning, you might find us more understanding than you think. Perhaps even helpful."

"Oh, but you are!" said Bron with feeling. "You've already been so, so helpful and now I feel we're being rude. Oh, I'm so tired, I don't know what I'm doing or saying."

All this while Oz and me stood there like a couple of idiots.

"Talking, talking!" said Stig. "What you need is sleep. Come with me."

So we found ourselves shortly on piles of hay in the outhouse with warm woollen blankets wrapped round us.

"We mustn't waste the candle," said Bron. "Let's blow it out and we can talk in the dark."

In the pitch black I just wanted to curl up and go to sleep, but Bron was insistent.

"What was all that about?" she asked. "You looked so shocked, Oz, I thought you'd seen a dead man walking."

"That's exactly what I did see," said Oz. "You didn't recognize him then?"

"No, should I?"

"But you did, didn't you, Wulf?"

"I did, but you were with him longer than me. You saw Gethin hang him."

"What?!" exclaimed Bron. "That was the boy Gethin hanged? So that was the boy in the sending today, with his face all rotting away."

"That's right," said Oz. "That's him. And now I know his name."

"You'd better tell me again what happened," said Bron. "I can't remember. I don't think you ever told me about it properly."

"It was so horrible," said Oz. "It'll stay with me for the rest of my life. But this...this...him turning up alive and everything. I can't take it in."

"But what happened?" persisted Bron.

I let Oz tell the tale although I was in a better state than him, because he'd actually been there from the beginning.

"Well," he started slowly. "Gethin needed someone to hang, for his horrible ceremony. So he'd grabbed this shepherd boy – I didn't know where he'd got him from – and made him a prisoner down in his dungeon where we were today, with all the skulls round the walls. But the thing was, he looked a lot like me: same height, same build, same colour hair. And when his men dragged me in there, we looked at each other and it was a bit like looking at reflections of ourselves in a pond.

"He was such an evil monster, Gethin. He made Stig and me change shirts, so I'd look even more like him and he'd look like me. Then his man set up this noose and we were both terrified. We both thought we were gonna be hanged. And they grabbed him first. He yelled and struggled, but they shoved his head in the noose, pulled the rope and that was that.

"I was nearly passing out when they grabbed me, but they just shoved me behind a curtain. And then they brought Wulf in."

I nodded. "Yeah. The body had its back to me and I saw it had Oz's shirt on, so I thought it was him. It was Gethin's idea of a joke. But then it swung round and they brought Oz out from behind the curtain. God, the relief! And then Gethin started his horrible ceremony. He had all the runes on the ground and they cut Oz's arm. It was bleeding quite a lot."

Oz gave a hollow laugh. "I remember," he said, "I thought, oh well, they're not gonna hang me, they're just gonna let me bleed to death."

"That's right," I said. "I started protesting, so then I had to give up my rune-stone or Gethin said he'd cut Oz to little pieces, only slowly. And he sprinkled Oz's blood over the runes – feeding them – he called it. And all the while the other boy's body was hanging there, swinging round. And then Gethin cut it down. He was saying stuff all the time, chanting stuff – I can't remember what.

"And then…oh God, it was horrible. The body started to jerk to its feet, like it did today. And Gethin asked it a couple of questions and it answered in this deep hollow voice."

"It was nothing like the boy's own voice," put in Oz.

"And Gethin was asking him stuff about whether he was going to be successful and the thing answered in a way that had two different meanings. I can't remember what the questions and answers were, can you, Oz?"

"No, I can't, but Gethin was such a cocky git that of course he took the answers to mean he'd be successful. But I can't remember a thing after that. I can only remember all this because Woden gave me my memories back, but that's where the memories end."

I nodded, but of course they couldn't see me in the pitch black.

"And that's when *I* was whirled back in time with Gethin, so I never saw the body again."

There was a pause.

Then, "Oh Diew," said Bronwen. "You've definitely never told me all that before. And you're sure Stig is the same boy?"

"Absolutely certain," said Oz.

Another silence, once again broken by Bron.

"You know, it's like when Abdul died and then was alive again. Do you remember, after the battle when I was on a cart going north, escaping from the Normans, we met Abdul on the road going south. I suppose he was going back to his beloved Andalucia. And we looked at each other and we knew we knew each other but we didn't know how. All those memories had been wiped out. So he was alive again, even though I'd seen him die. And now this boy, this Stig, is also alive when you saw him die."

More silence. Then I spoke.

"You know what? This is starting to make me feel just a little bit better. Ever since Woden gave me my memories back I've been blaming myself. Because I'd been whirled hundreds of years into the past with Gethin and when I arrived back in the present things had changed." I clenched my fists and a sour taste came into my mouth. I swallowed to get rid of it. "The Normans won." I took a deep breath. "But although that one big terrible thing did happen, a lot of *good* little things happened as well. Stig's alive when he would have had a nasty death, and it seems Abdul's alive too. It does make me feel just a *little* bit better."

Oz gave an enormous yawn.

"And you know what else?" said Oz. "I'm dropping off here. Let's shut up and go to sleep."

We slept late. The sun was well up when we opened the barn door. Hild and Edith were both working, out in the good autumn weather, Edith spinning wool into yarn and Hild thumping milk round in a wooden urn, churning it into butter. The sun shone on Hild's hair making it look buttercup yellow. I know Oz noticed that too. It was such a peaceful, homely scene, so different from what we'd been through the day before.

"I'll get you something to eat," said Edith.

"I'll help you," said Hild. "Glad to have a break; my arms are killing me."

We breakfasted outside on bread, ale and little bits of white sheep's cheese, while mother and daughter plied us with questions. In particular, Hild wanted to know how we'd stunned the two men. They were both so nice that I found myself telling them things I hadn't meant to, despite warning looks from the other two.

"The thing is," I said, "my mother was a wise-woman. Nothing bad, just healing people and stuff, though the priest didn't like her."

They both nodded knowingly.

"And she used runes," I went on. "I've got her rune-stones in a little bag. And she had this one very old rune-stone which I wear round my neck, and I found out it's quite a powerful protector. It can stun people who are attacking you."

Oz was looking more and more alarmed, but I wasn't going to show them Woden's runes or tell them anything about meeting him, let alone any of the other weird things that had happened to us. I'm not that daft. I drew my stone out from under my shirt and Hild nodded like mad.

"It's Thorn," she said to her mother. "I thought it would be Thorn or Eolh."

"Well done," said Edith. "Show them your staves, Hild."

Hild jumped up, ran into the cottage and came back with a small leather bag. She opened it and a pile of wooden staves spilled out on to the ground. On each of them was carved a rune. The shapes were a bit elongated because they'd been carved on to wooden sticks instead of round stones. But basically they were twenty-four rune-staves with exactly the same runes carved on them as my mum's rune-stones, as Woden's rune-stones.

"No priests round here," Hild grinned. "You're among friends."

CHAPTER TWENTY-FIVE

I've got to say I was surprised, though I don't know why. After all, my mum wasn't the only person to use runes. That's why the church was always going on about it. Anything to do with the old ways came straight from the devil according to them. Herbs, charms, anything. They wouldn't have got so worked up about it if there wasn't a lot of it still going on.

Another thing they did was change the words of charms and spells so they sounded Christian. But you couldn't really do that with runes. You could pretend they were just letters, a different alphabet, and they didn't have any magical meanings, but I didn't think Hild was using the runes to teach herself to read. As soon as you started to use them for guidance, or healing, or to tell the future, it was obvious that this was something right outside the church's power. And that meant trouble.

We all looked a bit stunned when the rune-staves were tipped out and Hild and Edith burst out laughing. I grinned at Edith.

"So are you a wise-woman then, like my mum?"

She laughed even more and shook her head, but Hild looked indignant. She put her hands on her hips and said, "Why don't you ask *me* that?"

"Well, you're a girl," I said.

"Oh, clever, aren't we. Great powers of observation you've got."

"No, I mean," I stuttered. "Of course you're a girl, but I just thought... Aren't you a bit young to be doing this stuff?"

Hild snorted, but Edith put her hand on her daughter's arm.

"I wonder how old your mother was when she started using the runes, Wulf. She must have had someone to teach her."

"I don't know," I said.

I felt really stupid because I suddenly realized I didn't know anything about when my mum was young. It was as if she'd sprung fully formed into the world to use the runes and give birth to me. How could I have been so lacking in curiosity? What an idiot I was! And of course she wasn't a great talker, my mum. She liked telling stories about the old gods, but I don't think she ever told me a story about herself. And I'd never asked! And now it was too late.

A picture of her lying there with the knife in her midriff floated unbidden into my mind and my eyes filled with tears. I turned away.

"Isn't that Stig coming back?" said Edith, standing up and looking in the opposite direction to me. Of course, everyone else looked that way too, giving me time to recover myself.

"Oh no, my mistake," she laughed, and by then I'd blinked myself back to normal. She was one of the most thoughtful people I've ever met, that woman.

"Anyway, it was my aunt who taught me," said Hild, who'd obviously decided to stop being annoyed. "Well, she *was* teaching me, until she died of the fever, so now I have to practise on my own."

"Yes, she thought Hild had a talent for it," said Edith, "just as Stigund has a magical way with animals. We all come into the world with our different abilities, and who's to say which ones are the most valuable?"

There was a pause, and then Hild said bluntly, "And I don't suppose you'll be wanting to tell us what you're doing in these parts?"

She raised her eyebrows and cocked her head to one side.

"Only if they want to, Hild," said Edith.

Hild ignored her mother. "But isn't it nice to repay a kindness with a story? After all, we did rescue you and feed you."

I was glad that Bron answered, because I didn't know what to say.

"You know how grateful we are, and we do trust you, but we can't really tell you absolutely everything." She paused. "But I think we can tell you quite a lot." She looked at me and Oz, but we sat there like a couple of ninnies.

"Right then," she went on. "We do know how evil Gethin was because we met him, but he's dead now."

"Thank goodness!" said Edith with feeling.

"I told you, Mum," said Hild. "You don't really trust the runes, do you. They said he was dead."

"Well, they were right," Bron went on. "But Madoc is trying to bring him back from the dead and we..."

She couldn't get any further because of Edith and Hild's expressions of horror.

"What!" "My God!" "This is worse than I imagined!"

When they'd calmed down a bit Bron carried on.

"And we have something Madoc thinks he needs to do that, to bring him back."

"What do you have?" asked Hild.

I finally found my voice.

"I'm really sorry, but I don't think we can tell you that just yet, though I hope we'll be able to one day."

Hild did one of her snorts but her mother said, "Leave it Hild. Just trust them."

Then Bron spoke again. "And the reason we're here is that we had to get this thing from Gethin's castle."

I guessed she was calling the runes a 'thing' to mislead them a bit about what they were.

"But what about the dragon?" asked Edith.

Then Oz found *his* voice. "Yeah, that's why Madoc couldn't get them...er, it. He waited for us to get it and then he attacked us. But thanks to you and your brother," looking at Hild, "he still hasn't got it...them... whatever. And we're still alive and free!"

So then of course all three of us thanked them again for what they'd done for us.

"That's fine," said Hild dismissively. "Never mind all that. How did *you* get into the castle with the dragon there?"

"Well, you see," said Bron. "I'd met the dragon before and..."

"You'd *met* the dragon!" exclaimed Hild. "What, did someone introduce you at the village fair?"

Me and Oz burst out laughing and Hild grinned back at us.

"Oh, long, long story, and nothing to do with this particular story," sighed Bron.

I thought the strain of this was starting to tell on her – I mean trying to explain what had happened without giving away too much.

"Bron was brilliant," I said. "The dragon doesn't speak English so Oz and me couldn't actually talk to her but Bron showed us how to bow to it and she did all the talking.

"And not only did it let us into the castle," I went on, "but it rescued us and got us out when things got really hairy."

"And did they get hairy!" said Oz. "You wouldn't believe all the magic spells Gethin left in that castle. I was amazed we got out alive."

"So that's why we're in this area," Bron finished off, "and that's why Madoc is after us."

Edith nodded. "This is serious," she said. "You obviously have to go away. That man is dangerous."

"We agree," I said. "But the trouble is we don't know where. We were hoping for a bit of guidance," *(Shut up! Don't mention Woden!)* "because we're not sure what to do next." *(And why don't you give us a bit of help, Woden?)*

"Well, guidance is what my runes are good at," said Hild, but she was interrupted by the puppy going wild, just as it had the night before when Stig was coming home.

Edith stood up. "That must be Stig coming back," she said, and this time it was.

But first came a bigger version of the black and white puppy. The little dog didn't know what to do with itself. It tore up and down, launched itself at its mother and then raced round and round. And when Stig himself appeared I thought it was going to die of ecstacy. He caught the puppy when it flung itself at him but his face was dead serious.

"You have to go. Now!" he said. "Madoc and his man have freed themselves and found horses. They're coming this way!"

CHAPTER TWENTY-SIX

Before I had time to take it in, Hild was on the ground scooping up her rune-staves and shoving them into their little bag.

"Follow me!" she ordered, and of course we did.

We were in unknown territory with not a clue where to hide, but Hild was on home ground. Besides, she had a natural authority despite her smiles and chattiness.

Oz skidded into the barn and came out with our bags and weapons, then we raced after Hild. She led us behind the cottage and down a slope to a wooded area. There she parted some undergrowth and said, "This'll have to do."

"What'll have to do?" said Oz, voicing my own thoughts.

Hiding in some bushes didn't seem likely to fool Madoc.

"Just go in and you'll see," said Hild impatiently.

We crouched down and squeezed through the opening and into a short passage a bit like a rabbit hole. And then we did see. The passage led us into a surprisingly roomy underground bolthole. There was no space to stand but we could sit comfortably. We weren't in complete darkness because although the walls and part of the roof were of earth, the rest of the roof was made of twigs. They were woven together so artfully that they looked quite natural, at least from below, and many were evergreen, so they gave good cover. The greenish light gave the place a slightly underwater feel.

"I'll leave you here," said Hild. "Be back when we've got rid of them."

But she was too late. The sound of hooves told us that Madoc and his man were already arriving.

"Better stay," whispered Hild, crawling in with us. "If I suddenly appear from this direction he'll start searching here."

Looking at Oz and Bron's tense faces I could see they were as nervous as me. The bolthole smelt strongly of earth and I felt slightly suffocated. Thank goodness for the twig roof. Never mind underwater: I began to feel as if I was in my grave. Bron suddenly did a couple of little gasps as if she was going to sneeze, but she clapped her hands over her face and managed to stifle the sound.

A horse whinnied and Madoc started to speak. Then we all knew how silent we had to be, for in the still morning air we could hear every word.

"And what are you doing here, shepherd, when you should be looking after my lord's sheep?"

"I came back for the puppy," answered Stig. "It's time he learned from his mother how to be a proper sheep dog. The sheep are all right without us for a bit."

Silence. Then Madoc barked an order. "Look in the hovel, and in that barn."

A grunt, and the sound of footsteps. I suddenly thought of our breakfast things, but surely Stig and Edith would have had the good sense to clear them away.

"But what are you looking for, my lord?" said Edith.

"Rather, *who* am I looking for," said Madoc. "And don't act the innocent. I am sure you know."

"Indeed no, my lord," said Edith. "We see few souls around here, being some way from the village."

"I am not talking of village idiots!" snapped Madoc. "Last night I was attacked. My men and I were waiting for three people who have stolen something belonging to my lord Gethin. These *thieves* had accomplices who killed some of my men and by some unnatural magic art escaped us."

The hypocrite! As if he didn't know anything about "unnatural magic arts"! And I noticed he didn't mention we'd knocked them out cold with our magic.

"Oh no, sir, how terrible!" gasped Edith. "Who could do such a thing?"

She was a really good liar – she almost convinced me. But she didn't convince Madoc. He looked straight at Stig.

"Their accomplices were two young men…about *your* height."

"There are lots of young men of my son's height," said Edith.

"The thieves and their accomplices are murderers," hissed Madoc. "When I catch them they will hang."

It suddenly came to me that we had no idea how much Madoc knew. Did he remember what happened before time changed its course? Did he remember hanging Stig? Was this some nasty game he was playing with Stig? Or did he simply know that Gethin was dead but not remember how it happened? At any rate he had somehow received a message from his dead master, telling him to get the runes. And presumably telling him how to bring Gethin back from the dead.

My gorge rose in my throat. I wanted this man dead as well as his master.

"Of course," Madoc went on, "anyone who could tell us the whereabouts of the three thieves might be treated more leniently."

Oh yeah?

"And you have another son, do you not?" he added.

"No, indeed, sir. I have a daughter."

"And where is she?"

"Off gathering firewood, sir. She should be back soon."

Hild frowned. I imagined she was regretting her decision to hide.

"And leaving her other chores half done, I see. Was she spinning or churning butter when it suddenly became urgent to gather firewood?"

"Oh that's me, sir. When my arms grow tired from the churning I take a little rest and do some spinning."

She was so cool, so unflustered! I was sure I couldn't have come up with such pat answers.

"There's nothing here, my lord," came the servant's voice. He had a strong Welsh accent but obviously spoke both languages, like Madoc. "Only these in a tub of water."

What were "these"?

"Oh, those are from our breakfasts, sir. Mine and my two children."

"Really?" sneered Madoc. "Surprising that such a good housewife would leave ale mugs in a tub of water, instead of washing and drying them."

"Well, it was such a nice morning that…"

"Enough!" bellowed Madoc. "I'm tired of your web of lies! Seize him!"

The dogs started barking so loudly that it was hard to hear what else was going on. But it didn't take much imagination. Then there was a yell and a cry of, "Call the monster off! Kill it, Gwyn!"

Hild grabbed my bow and arrows and ran up the tunnel.

CHAPTER TWENTY-SEVEN

Of course, me and Oz shot up the tunnel after her. What had we been so scared of? There only seemed to be two of them, though we hadn't known that at first. Then we were stopped in our tracks by a high-pitched yelp followed immediately by a long drawn out howl.

Hild bellowed like a warrior going into battle and tore round to the front of the cottage, nocking an arrow as she ran. We were hot on her heels and turned the corner in time to see Madoc's man collapse with an arrow in his leg while Stig and Madoc rolled on the ground. Stig was on top with a knife almost at Madoc's throat, while the howling went on, a heartwrenching animal cry. Then it stopped, followed by a deep, fierce growl, and the sheepdog leapt at the man with the wounded leg, who'd been doing a bit of bellowing himself. The man put up his hands to protect his face and the dog latched on to one of them. He yelled again and the dog shook the hand, growling all the time. She seemed to be doing all right on her own, so me and Oz both weighed in to help Stig.

But suddenly everything stopped.

A low chanting came from the throat threatened by Stig's dagger and the dagger itself froze in mid-air. Or rather, Stig froze, and the dog froze and we all found we couldn't move a muscle. Madoc pushed Stig off and he lay on his back with his arm still sticking up poised to strike. Edith stood in the doorway with a wooden staff in her hand, Oz was standing over Madoc with his sword arm raised and I was on the other side in the same position. Madoc brushed us off as he stood up, still chanting, and Oz toppled over. Hild was frozen in the act of nocking another arrow, and then I noticed Bronwen standing in the shadows. She'd come round the opposite side of the cottage and in her hand, now frozen like the rest of us, was the little knife she always carried.

All this had happened before, or something exactly like it. It hadn't been Madoc then but his master Gethin.

Slowly Madoc walked round till he stood in the middle of us, chanting all the while. Then he kicked something out of the way. A little black and white blood-stained heap of fur. And somehow that seemed like the worst thing. I moved my eyes to look at the puppy's mother, but she could no longer show what she was feeling. No more howls came from her throat, but I knew she was howling inside.

Madoc turned to look at each of us, an insufferable smile on his face even as his lips moved with the unknown words of the chant, and then… and then…his face began to change. Its features rippled, something moved under the skin, the eyes darkened. I watched in utter horror as Madoc became Gethin, became Madoc once again. His body twitched with the effort. The chanting finally stopped and the face settled into Gethin's.

"You see how powerful I am," said his deep voice, the voice I remembered so well. "I *will* possess those runes. I will return. My good servant Madoc will not be able to retrieve them now, until he recovers. This transformation, shall we say, takes it out of him." And he laughed.

What kind of master did this to a faithful servant? How could Madoc serve such a man?

"I must go now, but I will be back. We shall follow you wherever you go. The runes will be mine and then I shall be back for good."

The rippling began again. Madoc staggered and as his face became his own once more, but deadly white, he fell on to his hands and knees. He shuddered and retched a few times though nothing came out of his mouth. We were still frozen in the same positions and could only watch as he crawled toward his horse, heaved himself on to its back and slowly rode off with not a backward glance at us or his servant. He left the man to our mercy with no more thought than he'd given the dead puppy. With no more thought than Gethin had given him. Like master, like servant.

The sun rose to its midday height, carried on across the sky and we just stood, or lay, as we had been when the chanting started. I thought back to the last time this had happened. Gethin had been fighting Abdul on the hilltop and I'd been trying to stun with him with my rune, but

Abdul kept getting in the way. I'd already stunned one of Gethin's servants and the other lay dead with an arrow in him, this time shot by Bronwen. She was a really good shot, I remembered. But just as I'd thought I had a chance of knocking Gethin out, just as I'd begun to say the words, "By the power of Thorn…" he'd started this chanting. And we all froze. Just like now. Then Gethin had stuck his sword into Abdul's side and carted me off to join the imprisoned Oz, leaving Bron and Abdul like statues on the hillside.

Now the sun dipped lower in the sky and our shadows moved, but we didn't. Then I felt a twitching in my leg muscles. My sword arm started to ache and, "Ow, I've got cramp!" yelled Oz. Slowly life came back to our frozen limbs and I heard Madoc's man moaning. That seemed to remind the dog what she was doing and she bit his hand harder, so that the moan became a cry of pain.

"Get it off me," he yelled, and Hild shakily lowered the bow. She looked as if she'd been hit by a thunderbolt, and so did Stig, but she still managed to walk over to the injured man and give him a look that would have frozen a bubbling cauldron.

"That's what Madoc said, or something like that. But you didn't have to kill him. An innocent little puppy."

Stig picked himself up of the ground and shook himself.

"Leave him, Siggy! Come here, good dog."

Siggy obediently let go, after giving the hand one more shake, and started towards Stig. But then she saw her puppy, went and stood over him, lifted her head and sent one more howl up to the heavens. Stig crouched down and took the tiny body in one hand, while with the other he stroked its mother.

"We'll give him a proper burial, old girl," he whispered.

Siggy whimpered and gazed at her master with complete trust.

Everyone was coming back to life, but in an utter daze. It all seemed too much to take in, let alone talk about. Edith looked worse than anyone.

"What happened?" she gasped. "What just happened?"

No-one tried to answer as she looked round at us all. I just shook my head. Madoc's man looked completely terrified and started to edge away from us, but the arrow in his leg caught on the ground and he cried out.

Edith stared at him, then blinked and seemed to become her normal self. Still carrying the staff she went over to him and looked at the arrow sticking out of his calf. He started to shuffle away again.

"Keep still!" she snapped, finally dropping the staff. "Hild, come and give me a hand!"

"To do what?" asked Hild.

"Let's see if we can get this arrow out. And I suppose I'd better see to his hand as well."

"What?" said Hild. "But he's the enemy! If it was up to him and Madoc we'd *all* be dead, not just the puppy."

"No," moaned the man. "That's not true. You have to do what he says. You don't know what he's like."

"Puh!" spat Hild. "That's no excuse. I think we *do* know what he's like, but I'd never do his bidding!"

Bron had quietly walked over and stood looking down at him.

"Your name's Gwyn, isn't it?" she said. "I thought I heard him call you Gwyn."

The man nodded.

"I'll help, if you like," Bron went on. "Though heaven knows he doesn't deserve it."

"Thank you, Bronwen," said Edith, ignoring her daughter. "See, I think he's lucky. The arrow's gone almost through his calf, so if we can just push it through to the other side, then we can break it and pull the head out one way and the shaft out the other."

Ouch, I thought. *He's getting his punishment.*

Me and Oz looked at each other. I felt completely unnecessary, as if I might as well not be here, and I think Oz felt the same. But it was good to see the rest of them doing things, coming out of the weird atmosphere left behind by the enchantment.

"If I'd been able to get a better shot I'd have done more than get his calf," said Hild. "But I couldn't get a good aim, with the dogs and Stig in the way."

"Never mind that," said Edith. "Hild, you know where I keep my linen and herbs, and we'll need water."

Hild rolled her eyes and went to the cottage, and Bron crouched down to look at the wound. But suddenly she gave a little cry and stood up again, staring straight ahead. We all looked where it seemed she was looking, but there was nothing there, just the cottage wall.

I jumped up. "What is it, Bron? What's the matter?"

She didn't answer, but stood as frozen as we all had been a little while ago.

I grabbed hold of her.

"What's happened?" I said frantically, and she collapsed in my arms.

CHAPTER TWENTY-EIGHT

But as soon as I felt her falling against me, as soon as I clasped her to me in a way I dreamed of but never dared in real life, she jerked awake. She pushed me away, shook her head and started gasping and flailing around as if she'd been drowning.

"Bron, what is it?" I said, like an idiot.

"She's had one of her visions," said Oz, matter-of-factly. "Let's hope she's come back with some clear instructions about what we're supposed to do next." He paused, while Bron blinked and her breathing slowed to something more normal.

"A map would be good, too," Oz went on.

"Shut up!" I snapped.

I agreed with him, but how could he stay so calm? I couldn't think about all that until I knew Bron was all right.

Which she seemed to be.

"I'm so sorry!" she gasped. "Was I like it for long?"

"No time at all," said Edith soothingly. "Here, come and sit down. Have something to eat and drink. It'll ground you."

Edith guided Bron to the stool by the spinning wheel, while Hild rushed to bring her some bread and watered ale. Bron accepted it gratefully and took a few long sips. We'd all gathered round, even Siggy the dog, and were waiting eagerly for her to explain. Even Madoc's man, Gwyn, lying there in pain, looked as if he wanted to know what was going on.

"It seemed to me as if I was gone a long time," said Bron at last. "I was miles away from here, back at Grimwold's hall. It was horrible to be back there." She paused and looked at Edith, Stig and Hild. "You three don't know who Grimwold was."

Then she shook her head and shut her eyes. I was afraid she wasn't going to be able to carry on, but she took a deep breath and opened them again. "Grimwold was another sorceror, a bit like Gethin, but he was an English lord, and he also was collecting these runes that Gethin wants."

She took another breath and looked almost apologetically at Edith, Stig and Hild.

"We didn't make it clear what this treasure was that we are carrying. I'm sorry about that, but sometimes it seems wiser not to tell everything. It's not that we didn't trust you but…Anyway, you all know now that we have some precious rune-stones which are the thing Gethin needs to bring him back to life. Back to life properly, I mean, not just using Madoc's body." She shuddered and took another sip. "And *that* was horrible too, wasn't it, seeing his face in Madoc's? Anyway, you know now that it was rune-stones because Gethin said so himself. But we don't have a complete set and I saw in my vision where the other runes are."

I nodded. "They're at Grimwold's place, aren't they?"

"Yes," said Bron. "But Wulf, it's dangerous there. I could find them, I saw where they're hidden. The hall is still a burnt ruin, the way we left it, but the difference now is…the Normans are there. Some of their soldiers are using it as a base, the bits that weren't destroyed in the fire. If we want to get the rest of the rune-stones we have to go right back into Norman territory."

"So why do we have to get them back?" asked Oz. "It's Gethin that wants them, not us. We could just hand over the ones we've got."

"Hand them over to who?" said Stig. "There's *still* a lot you're not telling us."

"We will," I said, "though it'll strain your powers of belief, but now's not the time."

"No, but Oz," Bron shook her head. "The awful thing is, I had this really, really strong feeling, in my vision, that that's what we're supposed to do."

She looked at us helplessly and my heart sank. I remembered the massive hall and the gallows built in the courtyard. I remembered the two figures tied to posts waiting to be hanged: Abdul with his head lolling, so badly beaten up, Bron trying to be brave, both of them with their lips moving in prayer. In my heart I thanked the elves who'd helped us rescue them. They'd set the stables alight so we could all escape in the chaos. And they'd helped me kill Grimwold when *he* was trying to kill *us*. In my mind's eye I could see the elf-fire leaping from roof to roof, impossible to put out. And now Bron was saying we had to return there. By the look on her face it was the last thing in the world that she wanted to do.

"Well, I think none of us can stay *here* for a while," said Hild. "Even you, Mum. Madoc'll be back."

"What, leave my home?" said Edith, horrified.

Hild put her arm round her mother. "Go and stay with Aunt Emma, just till it's all blown over."

"Good idea," said Stig. "But I'm not going anywhere."

"Why not?" said Edith and Hild together.

"I can't leave the sheep. Winter's coming and wolves. After that it's lambing. Siggy and I need to stay."

"Well, I think a load of old sheep can look after themselves!" exploded Hild. "What did they do before humans started looking after them?"

"Got eaten by wolves and died when the lambing went wrong."

"I give up!" said Hild in exasperation. "Anyway, I'm going to consult *my* runes, see if they can tell us what to do."

She stalked off inside the cottage.

"Leave her," said Edith. "The runes always calm her down, and perhaps she *will* have some guidance."

"So," said Stig, "see to your prisoner, Mum. Siggy and I will go and bury the pup, and then I think you all ought to gather what you can take with you and decide where to go."

And Stig too walked away, the faithful Siggy at his heels, off to the woods behind the cottage.

We all looked at Gwyn, who shuffled away a bit. We'd almost forgotten him and I actually felt a bit sorry for him. Edith herself went in to fetch the linen, herbs and water that she needed, while Bron sat unmoving, her face a picture of misery and dread. I smiled at her, rather pathetically, trying to cheer her up.

*

It had been a fine late autumn day but now the sun was dipping near the horizon and the shadows were long.

"Let's get this done while we've still got a bit of light," said Edith, and she made Gwyn shift around so that his leg was in the evening sunlight. Then she and Bron knelt over the wound with the arrow in it.

Oz beckoned me and we withdrew into the shadow of the outhouse, where we could talk without being overheard.

"What are we gonna to do?" I moaned.

"*I* don't know," said Oz. "Where's your precious Woden when we need him?"

There was an almighty yell, as Edith tried to push the arrow through to the other side of Gwyn's calf.

"Serves him right!" said Oz.

"Never mind that," I said. "Look, Bron's always been right before."

"Except when she thought Abdul was our enemy," grunted Oz.

"Which you never let her forget," I said. "But she was younger then and after that she never got a single thing wrong when she had her visions."

We leant against the wall in a silence broken by moans and then one ear-splitting yell.

"That's it, we're through," said Edith triumphantly. "Now if I can just cut this arrowhead off you can pull at the shaft."

"Oh, no," moaned Gwyn. "Can't we have a rest?"

"Let's get it over with," said Bron curtly. "You should be grateful we're not leaving you with an arrow sticking out of your leg."

"I think I'd rather have that," pleaded Gwyn.

"Don't be a baby," said Bron, which made Oz snigger.

"Hope she never has to see to one of *my* wounds," he grinned. It was a relief to see Bron doing something practical, and forgetting her vision for the moment. Then Oz turned to me.

"You know what? I wouldn't mind going back and killing a few Normans. I've never been happy with what Woden said. You know, that we should leave the war, it's basically lost and all that."

"Oz," I shook my head. "I feel the same about that, you know I do, but if we do go back we won't be fighting. We'll have to sneak around, lie really low and just somehow get the runes back."

"What, not even a few arrows in the bastards?"

"Not unless we have to. We'll have Bron with us as well. Remember what happened to her last time we were there? She nearly got hanged. We'll have to protect her."

Oz looked gloomy. "I don't think Norman soldiers would bother with hanging. It'd just be a sword through your gut."

"Yeah," I said. "So we'd have to try to be invisible, stay alive, get the runes and hope that Woden finally shows himself. Or sends the ravens or something."

"We've gotta take Bron," sighed Oz, "'cos she knows where the things are."

I nodded, but another yell made us both turn our heads to see Gwyn rolling around in agony and Bronwen holding aloft the bloody headless arrow.

"Got it!" she grinned, while Edith poured some water on the wound and wrapped it tightly with strips of linen. I grinned too, happy to see Bron smile.

"Got what?" asked Hild, coming out of the cottage. "Oh, that. I don't know why you bothered. More importantly, I've just had one of the clearest rune readings I've ever had. It was as if they were speaking to me. And they told me, yes, you've got to go back east, you three. And they also told me that I'm coming with you."

CHAPTER TWENTY-NINE

"Oh no, Hild!" cried Edith. "First you tell me I have to leave my home and then you say you're leaving me as well."

And she burst into tears.

The evening went by in a blur, with Hild and Stig arguing, Bron helping Hild get stuff ready, Hild and Stig arguing again and Edith sobbing her heart out. It was funny – she'd been so cool and calm when Madoc was questioning her but she went to pieces at the thought of going away. Probably the day's mad events had taken their toll as well.

One thing we did make sure of was finding out as much as we could from Gwyn. How many men did Madoc have, where was his base, that sort of thing. Bronwen washed and wrapped his dog-mangled hand in linen and questioned him in Welsh. Oz wasn't too happy about that. He thought we might miss some vital bit of information, but I knew why Bron was doing it. She was being a bit more friendly to him than she had been and you could see him gradually relax. He was opening up, speaking his native tongue, telling her quite a lot.

It turned out Madoc had based himself in a small fort on the borders a little way north of here. He only had about thirty or forty men, most of whom had been Gethin's. Apparently a lot of Gethin's men had run away when he disappeared and weird things started happening in the castle. I couldn't blame them. I'd have run a mile.

"And he's lost a few *more* men now, thanks to Hild and Stig," grinned Oz.

Gwyn was one of the few who Madoc had rounded up from local villages. He was planning to go home if he could and I didn't blame him for that, either. Madoc had abandoned Gwyn so why should he feel any loyalty to him?

"Rest your leg for a day," sniffed Edith. "There's food here and you've still got your horse, so you can go home then." She paused. "But are you sorry for joining up with that evil man? I bet killing the pup is the least of what you've done, working for him."

Gwyn looked sheepish.

"I never would have gone with him if I'd known what it was going to be like. But once he's got you in his power it's hard to get away."

Hild stared coldly at him and turned to Stig once more.

"I think you're being really selfish. Mum'll be worried sick with you staying here."

"I'm not going to stay *here*, am I? I'll be in the hills with the sheep. You know how I can hide away, practically make myself invisible. I'm not going to put on a bright red tunic and dance around yelling for Madoc to come and get me! And Siggy's a good dog. She knows when she has to stay quiet. And what about you? Don't you think Mum's going to be worried about you? Why don't you go to Aunt Emma's with her?"

"Because the runes told me I have to go with the others!"

"The runes!" said Stig in disgust. And he went to sort out his own belongings.

Oz had been following all this with enormous interest. I'd seen his face light up when Hild said she was coming, and I'd seen it fall when Stig suggested she should go with Edith. It was clear he was smitten.

But I was a bit worried. Did Bron like Hild? How would they get on if they had to spend a lot of time together? It was bad enough when Oz and Bron started bickering. We didn't need any more of that. I realized I was feeling really protective of her. I couldn't blame Oz for how he felt about Hild, because I felt just the same about Bron, although I'd known her a lot longer than he'd known Hild. But when I looked at Bron I sort of thought it would be all right. She wasn't the girl I'd known two years ago. She was more grown up than any of us. Bronwen had become a woman.

Eventually Edith was persuaded to go through things with Hild and decide what she could take and what had to be left. I went and stood in the cottage doorway and asked if I could help. But actually I wanted a last look at the place which had been so briefly our safe haven. Was it only last night we'd had that delicious mutton stew?

I could see why Edith was so upset. This place was a real home, cosy in a way my own home had never been. The floor was swept, everything was tidy and there was even a woollen wall hanging, probably worked by Edith. Oz's cottage had been full to overflowing with kids, but mine had been, well…a little bit lacking in homeliness. I'd never realized – it was all I'd ever known, and I was well-fed and had enough basic clothes to wear. The best bits had been in the evenings when Mum had told Oz and me stories about the old gods. We'd loved that. But still…it somehow hadn't been as homely as this place.

By now it was dusk.

"I think you can risk one more night here," said Stig, "but we must leave before dawn. I'll come with you as far as Aunt Emma's village."

Edith's eyes started to well up again and Stig put his arm round her.

"Don't worry, Mum, I'll be able to come by and see you. Everyone there knows us, no-one'll give us away."

"Thank you, Stig," sniffed Edith, and we had a quick supper and all bedded down for the night. Then in the morning, when it had barely started to get light, we picked up our bags and weapons and set off. Bron and Edith said goodbye to Gwyn but the rest of us couldn't be bothered.

Edith's sister lived not in the next village but one a fair few miles further on, so we spent the rest of that day together. Edith had given us good provisions – bread (which would soon go stale), cheese, plenty of dried meat and flasks of both milk and ale, the milk to be drunk first. Me and Oz had never been so well-stocked.

Emma welcomed us all and that evening she and her family listened open-mouthed to Edith's tale. We'd agreed she should say Madoc had turned nasty and accused them of stealing Lord Gethin's sheep. Everyone knew the penalty for sheep stealing was hanging, so that would explain our flight from the cottage.

The next morning was hard for Edith and for Hild, who obviously wasn't as tough as she liked to appear. But finally, with a goodbye woof from Siggy, the four of us were on our way. Back to the flatter lands of south-east England, where Hild had never been. Back to Grimwold's hall, which held such horrible memories for Bronwen. And back to the Normans.

We knew which general direction to go in because of following the sun. We could all do that. But what did you do if there was no sun? If it didn't break though the cloud cover all day? We relied on Bron. She had an uncanny sense of direction, observing the clouds, the wind, moss on trees, which way the birds were flying. It was as if she herself was part of nature. When I told her this she looked puzzled.

"But of course, Wulf," she said. "We're all part of nature, just as much as that hawk hovering in the sky...or the fieldmouse on the ground that he's searching for."

I thought I'd rather be a hawk than a fieldmouse.

So the next day, which was grey and murky, we followed Bron's lead. Hild was obviously impressed with Bron's ability to read natural signs and it was a relief that the two girls seemed to be getting on. When we stopped for the night Hild started showing Bron how to use a sword. Not the long swords that Oz and I had, but the shorter seax.

She'd say things like, "See, you won't have the reach of your opponent, but you can duck underneath and stab with yours. Like...*this*!"

And she felled her pretend opponent with a flourish, making Oz and me roar with laughter. She didn't mind, though. She was grinning herself.

I was pleased. Bron was already a good shot with a bow and arrow and she was enjoying this. Though it'd take a lot of practice before she could wield her seax well enough to actually protect herself. And it was good that someone her own height was teaching her. Somehow, in the two years since we'd last met, me and Oz had shot up so that now I looked down at her. How did that happen? We used to be the same height!

"How did you come to have two seaxes, Hild?" asked Oz.

"One was my dad's and Stig picked up the other, on one of our little skirmishes – against rustlers trying to steal our sheep."

That made sense but still, it was unusual for a shepherding family to own weapons like that and I'd noticed, when Stig gathered his belongings together, that he had a proper sword, like Oz's and mine. We'd been given ours by Guthlac, our commander, when he'd decided we deserved them and we wouldn't be likely to let them fall into the hands of an enemy. Swords were precious things, even plain ones like ours, and to a lesser extent so were seaxes. It made me wonder if there was something we didn't know about Stig and Hild.

The next day it rained non-stop and we got soaked through. We kept to wooded land as much as we could, but that wasn't much protection as the trees were now bare of leaves. Luckily the weather dried out after that, but it was cold and grey. Winter was coming.

We spent a bit of time hunting as we wanted to make the dried meat and cheese last. I was worried about slowing down because I was sure Madoc would be after us with some men when he'd recovered, but we tried to leave no trail behind us. And all the time we were keeping an eye out for Normans.

Signs of them grew more and more frequent. Burnt out villages and farmsteads, slaughtered livestock, but no soldiers. Until one evening Bron – of course, it would be Bron – told us to hush and put her ear to the ground. It made me shiver. It was exactly what my mum had done just before she died.

"I hear hooves," she said.

"Which direction?" asked Oz.

Bronwen frowned and shook her head. "I'm not sure," she said. Then, "Yes, I am. They're coming from both directions, behind us and in front."

CHAPTER THIRTY

Hild's eyes widened, as we all took it in.

"So we're trapped," she said.

"No we're not," said Oz. "There's got to be somewhere we can hide!"

"Shush!" hushed Bronwen. "I'm still listening!"

Her eyes were closed as she laid one ear to the ground, an intent expression on her face. Then she splayed both hands on the earth as well, as if her fingers were extra ears.

"There are not that many behind us and they're still some way off. But travelling fast, I think."

"Madoc's men," said Oz grimly, voicing my own thoughts.

"But a lot in front…it sounds like an army!"

Hild had been looking round desperately.

"Over there!" she pointed. "Let's get there quick!"

There was a small settlement a few hundred yards away and it looked deserted.

"It's a bit obvious," said Oz, "and it may not be as deserted as it looks."

"All right then, clever boots," said Hild. "Got a better idea?"

"Maybe," I said. "Look over there."

"Where?" said Oz, following the direction I was pointing. "There's nothing there."

"In the sky," I whispered.

Two black birds were wheeling around each other, making acrobatic circles just below the clouds.

The girls still didn't understand, but Oz's face lightened with a glimmer of hope.

"But it might not be them," he said.

"I know," I nodded. "But I have this feeling…and we'd better move quickly. Trust us," I said to Hild and Bron.

Hild's face showed not one ounce of trust, but she shrugged and followed on as we scrambled across muddy fields in the direction of the wheeling birds. As we got closer we could see that they were indeed ravens and I sent up a silent prayer of thanks to Woden. Though I knew, of course, that they might be two completely different birds and not Huginn and Muninn at all. Ravens mate for life and this could just be a pair having fun with each other. Still…I had this feeling. And it was about time Woden did something for us!

The land looked flat but it was criss-crossed with ditches which you couldn't see until you were practically on top of them. I started to feel uneasy, and not just about being caught between Madoc's men and the Normans. All along, at the back of my mind I'd been wondering whether we might come across my mum's temporary grave. Her *very* temporary grave. When we'd left her body curled up under the cart, I'd thought we might be able to come back in a day or two and bury her properly, but now a bit more than a day or two had passed. I didn't want to think what state her body might be in. I didn't really want to come upon her lying there in the ditch, under the cart that had led to her death. But this landscape was looking horribly similar to where we'd left her.

Then as we ran and stumbled across the fields I noticed a mound, an unusually green mound all on its own in the flat fields. I was so surprised that I stopped, until Oz grabbed my arm and tugged me on.

And then there was a sudden dip which had us running and skidding downhill until we reached level ground again. I looked back, but the mound was out of sight. Ahead of us, however, and completely hidden from the higher ground where we'd been before, was a little wood. The ravens circled round, getting closer and closer and finally landing on the bare branches of a beech tree. One of them cawed loudly at us and I recognized the harsh *cark, cark*. You might think one raven sounds exactly the same as another, at least to human ears, but I knew this one. His cry had filled my ears when Woden was making me remember what had happened to us.

Oz was grinning all over his face and I realized that it was that same sound that had brought back his memories too. Relief flooded through me and I forgot all about the mound.

"Thanks Muninn," said Oz. And when the other bird squawked indignantly, he added, "Oh, and you too Huginn. I wasn't forgetting you."

Hild's face had drained of colour and she clutched Oz's arm.

"Huginn? Muninn?" she whispered. "I don't believe it."

"Well, you'd better believe it," I grinned. "We did tell you."

We had tried to tell Hild the long, complicated story of our adventures each evening as we'd eaten and rested. But it was a lot to take in and I knew it would strain the belief of most people. Of course, Hild wasn't most people – she read the runes and knew all the old stories. But still… to meet Woden's ravens herself!

Then I looked at Bron. She was studying the birds with a gentle smile on her face. She hadn't known our old tales, apart from what we'd told her, but it seemed to me that she was connecting with them in some wordless way. What an incredible person she was.

I hated to break the spell, but it seemed daft to stay out in the open.

"Come on," I said, "let's get under cover."

And we walked into the little wood in a kind of trance. Although the trees were bare of their own leaves they were thickly covered with ivy and there were holly bushes around as well. A rich, loamy smell filled our nostrils from the mouldering leaves under our feet and the whole place had a quiet, magical air so that you felt you had to speak in whispers. The loudest sound was the ravens hopping from branch to branch, leading us on into the centre of the wood. They stopped when they reached a clearing and we collapsed on the ground, exhausted.

I gazed up at the great birds and they stared back at me, their bright eyes as black as their feathers, as black as their huge, dangerous looking beaks. Impossible to read what was going on in their heads.

"Are you staying with us now?" I asked. "Are you going to show us the way."

Not a sign. They just glared at me.

"Well," said Oz, "I reckon it's time to eat."

So we shared out our increasingly meagre rations and ate, too weary to say anything much. Hild never once took her eyes off Huginn and Muninn. As dusk fell, and the birds hunkered down on their branch and closed their eyes, our eyes closed too. Slowly we curled up where we were and fell sleep.

Early next morning the branch was bare. The ravens were gone. I stared up at the pale chilly sky through the boughs of the trees and wondered if they were going to come back. I doubted it. I was disappointed but not surprised. They'd saved us from being squashed between Madoc's men and the Norman army and I supposed that was their job done.

Then I realized that we had a visitor. Oz and Hild were still asleep, wrapped in their cloaks, next to each other but a yard apart. Bron however was awake and smiling, resting on one elbow. With her other arm she was beckoning to something. Something I couldn't see. She seemed to be looking at an ivy-covered tree trunk, but when I stared in that direction I realized there was a tiny person there. And when I say tiny I mean less than a foot high. Her green eyes were so big they almost filled her face, her curly hair was greenish and so was her flimsy dress. You had to look quite hard to make her out against the ivy. She was half smiling back at Bronwen as if trying to make up her mind about her.

Then I did the most stupid thing you could think of.

"Hello," I said, "who are you?"

She looked at me aghast, yelped and ran back into the trees.

"Oh, well done, Wulf," said Bron. "You've terrified her."

"I didn't think I was that ugly," I said.

Bronwen shook her head, but couldn't help grinning.

But who was this little person? She was so much smaller than the elves we'd met in the past. She could only be a very young elf child.

Which it seemed that she was, because in no time at all she reappeared in the arms of what seemed to be her mother.

But I knew her!

And so did Bron!

We beamed a welcome and the young mother yelled, "Toadstool! Mugwort! Here they be!"

CHAPTER THIRTY-ONE

Oz and Hild woke up with a start, as Bron and I shouted, "Bramble!"

Bramble marched grinning into the clearing, with her daughter burying her face in her shoulder.

"Well," she said. "'Tis a while since we seen you, and there's two here I ain't never met. Leastways, I *seen* you, Oz, though you ain't seen me, but we ain't none of us met this other young maid."

Oz looked a bit nonplussed at this, but just then Mugwort and Toadstool came bounding into the glade. They too had smiles big enough to split their faces and Oz leapt over, fell on his knees and hugged them both.

"Here!" spluttered Toadstool, pushing him off. "Thass enough o' that! I ain't lived all these years to be crushed to death by a human!"

Bramble, Bron and me were doubled up laughing, but Hild sat there with her mouth wide open.

"Tryin' to catch flies?" said Mugwort, shaking himself after Oz's bone-crushing hug.

Hild shut her mouth quickly. "It's just…it's just…" she mumbled, but couldn't get any further.

"I wasn't meanin' to be rude," said Mugwort, "but you did look a bit funny. But I 'specks you ain't never seen an elf before."

"No," said Hild, finding her voice. "And this comes straight after meeting Woden's two ravens. It's all a bit…a bit…"

Looking at Hild I remembered how me and Oz had reacted when we first saw the elves. Now we greeted them as good friends, but then we'd been stunned to see these stocky little brown and green people, about three feet or so high, with their snub noses, slanted eyes and big pointed ears. It had taken us a while to accept that we actually were looking at *elves.*

"Thass a'right," said Bramble soothingly to Hild. "Don' pay them no mind. 'Tis always a shock to a young elf child when they first sees a human. I keeps Thistle away when I can but she have seen one or two."

At the mention of her name, Thistle lifted her face away from her mother's shoulder and stuck her thumb in her mouth. She looked gravely at each of us, sucking so hard that I thought the thumb might drop off.

"Well, I thinks we should all interduce ourselves," said Bramble, "seein' as how we doesn't all know each other."

"Hang on there, Bramble," said Toadstool. "How's about a bit o' breakfast? We can talk an' eat at the same time."

"If you ain't too pertickler about us talkin' wi' our mouths full," put in Mugwort, and he produced a leather bag out of which he pulled a number of plucked and roasted little birds. Maybe quail, judging by their size.

"That's fine," said Oz. "I'm famous for talking with my mouth full."

"Oh, thank you," said Bron. "Our rations are getting a bit low."

There was a bird each and a couple left over and we all set to with a will.

"Is this your wood?" I asked, though I should have known better.

"Depends what you means," said Mugwort. "If you means, does we live here, then the answer is, some o' the time. But if you means, does we own it, then I'd a thought you'd a known the answer to that."

"Thass the trouble wi' humans," said Bramble, ripping off a piece of meat and giving it to Thistle.

"Thass *one* o' the problems wi' humans," put in Mugwort. "They always got to go on about ownin' things. How can you own a wood? The wood owns itself. That there tree owns itself, don't it?"

I nodded. "I suppose I meant, do you live here, and you've answered that."

"Look," said Bramble impatiently. "We ain't interducin' ourselves! I'll start. I'm Bramble, an' I met Wulf an' Bronwen when they was lookin' for Oz. 'Cos Oz, he was kep' prisoner by that evil Gethin, an' thass why

I never met him. And this here's Toadstool," Toadstool bowed, "and this here's our baby daughter Thistle."

Thistle stopped eating for a moment and turned her face once more towards her mother's shoulder. But the meat was obviously too tempting, so she turned back and went on chewing at it.

Then it was Toadstool's turn. "I'm Toadstool and me an' Mugwort an' a load of our friends met Wulf an' Oz when Pooka captured 'em. But then he let 'em go an' we all wen' and rescued Bronwen here from that other evil human, that Grimwold. Her an' that human wi' a brown face like our'n. What were his name?"

"Abdul," I said.

"Thass right. He had a beautiful black horse. Anyroad, thass how I knows three of you."

"An' I'm Mugwort, an' I knows you three from all that, but then I helped Wulf when he was kep' prisoner by that Gethin."

"Let me tell them about that," I interrupted excitedly. Because it was all coming back to me and I sat there eating their breakfast and feeling full of love for them all. I turned to Hild, who hadn't said a word.

"You know who Gethin is don't you? He's the one who wants all the rune-stones to bring him back to life. *You* remember – Madoc's face turned into his."

"Of course I remember," said Hild a bit huffily. "Who could ever forget a thing like that? But what *you* seem to be forgetting is that I've known Gethin longer than you have!"

"Oh yeah, sorry," I mumbled, feeling stupid.

"Hang on, hang on!" said Toadstool. "Woss' this about his face?"

"We'll explain in a minute," I said. "I just want to tell Hild what a wonderful thing Mugwort did."

And I told the story of how Mugwort taught me to concentrate on my rune-stone and how I found myself in Woden's forest and how Woden charged me to stop Gethin turning back time, as he planned to do.

"It was so brave of Mugwort, *and* Pooka, to get into Gethin's castle and come to my room. They airflitted in, Hild, through all these dark spells, to help me."

"Airflitted?" said Hild.

"They just vanish in one place and reappear in another," I tried to explain.

"It were hard gettin' through all them spells," nodded Mugwort.

"Anyway, *he's* the one who taught me to concentrate on my runestone so that I found myself in this forest with Woden! And Woden told me how to defeat Gethin. But if it hadn't been for Mugwort I couldn't have done it."

It was lucky I'd already told Hild a lot of this or she wouldn't have had a clue what I was going on about. But I was so excited about seeing the elves again, having them right here in front of me, that it was hard to explain things properly.

"Right," said Toadstool. "Now I reckon it be the maid's turn to interduce herself, and p'raps while she's at it she can tell us about this here thing wi' Gethin's face."

Hild looked around at us all and, for the first time in ages she smiled.

"Well, I'm Hild, and I haven't known the others long. In fact, me and my brother did a bit of rescuing ourselves, when these three were captured by Madoc and his men."

"Yeah," said Oz, "they were great! We thought Hild was a boy because of how she was dressed and she's amazing with a bow and arrow. And a sword, too. But of course, we could see she was a girl as soon as she uncovered her face."

Hild beamed at him.

"Anyway, they came back to my Mum's place," she went on, "but the next day Madoc turned up."

"You keeps talkin' about this Madoc, but we don' rightly know who he be," said Mugwort.

"Sorry," I said, "he's Gethin's right-hand man and he's in charge of getting Woden's runes so he can bring him back from the dead."

At this there was a lot of tutting among the elves.

"That don' sound good," said Toadstool, shaking his head.

"But the thing is," Hild went on, "while he was there, a horrible sort of change came over his face. It kind of rippled, and then it looked like somebody else. Somebody with really evil eyes. Then I recognized Gethin. And his voice changed too. It got really deep and he said something like, 'We shall follow you wherever you go. The runes will be mine and I shall be back for good!' And when Madoc went back to normal he collapsed and hardly had the strength to crawl over to his horse."

Toadstool and Mugwort shook their heads and whistled.

"This be real bad," said Toadstool.

"And where be these runes?" asked Mugwort.

"I had a vision," said Bron. "They're back at Grimwold's estate, so that's where we're heading."

There was a lot more headshaking and muttering, but I noticed that Bramble's brown face went paler, and she clutched Thistle to her.

"Well, we can take yous all there the safest ways," said Mugwort, "but we ain't goin' inside."

"An' I ain' goin' nowhere near that evil place," wailed Bramble. "An' I doesn' want you to neither, Toadstool! After all what happened there! Never mind ol' Woden an' his runes – I don' think *none* o' yous should go there, or yous all won't get out alive!"

CHAPTER THIRTY-TWO

Toadstool hugged Bramble to him and little Thistle started to wail in sympathy.

"There, there, both o' yous. Shush, shush," soothed Toadstool. "Ain't no harm goin' to come to none of us."

The mood had changed completely and there was nothing we could do but sit and watch. But I knew why Bramble was so upset.

She and her big sister Thistle, who this little one was obviously named after, had been exploring near Grimwold's place. He had captured Thistle, though Bramble had managed to hide, but she'd seen what happened. Grimwold had used black spells to stop Thistle escaping and then he'd *hanged* her. He'd actually *hanged* the little elf as part of a dark ceremony. Bramble had escaped and told the rest of the clan, but she was so shattered that she'd just wandered off and no-one could find her. Toadstool had been in love with Thistle, so he eventually set off and looked high and low until he found Bramble. Then he gradually grew to love her and she him and this baby was the result.

Of *course* Bramble would be terrified of going back there.

"Can't you just tell us the way," I said, "if Bramble's so upset? Or maybe Mugwort could show us which paths to take."

"That be right thoughtful, Wulf," replied Toadstool. "But see I don't reckon 'twere no accident them ravens led you here. I reckon we was *meant* to find you. We bin talkin' a bit about you an' we reckoned somethin' funny were goin' on."

"You mean," said Oz, "*Woden* meant you to find us?"

"Ooh, I didn' mean that ezackly," Toadstool shook his head. "He ain't the king o' this world, tho' he like to think he be."

"He be very powerful an' all that," put in Mugwort, "but there be deeper powers than his'n. Even Woden be part o' the web o' Wyrd. Them ravens knowed they was doin' the right thing bringin' you here, and they was, because they saved you from all them other humans, but they might not a' knowed *we* was here."

"So how did *you* know about us escaping the Normans, and Madoc's men?" asked Hild.

"Oh, you learns a lot, airflittin'," said Toadstool.

"An' jus' keepin' all your senses open," said Mugwort.

Bramble had stopped sobbing, but she still clung tightly on to Toadstool and Thistle.

"Why can't he go an' get his own runes, that ol' god," she sniffed, "'stead o' puttin' other folks in danger? Other folks what ain't done nobody no harm?"

"Good question," I said bitterly. "I've asked him that myself and all he said was, his powers in middle earth – that's here – aren't as great as they were when everybody used to worship him."

Bramble did a cross between a snort and a hiccup.

"But we've got to do it, Bramble," I went on. "We can't risk Madoc getting the rest of the runes first and bringing Gethin back. We just need a pointer in the right direction. *You* don't have to go anywhere near the place."

"And the sooner we starts the better," said Mugwort, "wi' yous all goin' so slow. 'Tis a right shame humans can't airflit."

"Well, I'll come the first bit," sniffed Bramble, "but thass all."

So we packed up our few belongings and followed the elves. *We* might not have been able to airflit but it turned out to be really useful that the elves could. Either Toadstool or Mugwort would flit ahead to make sure the coast was clear and I started to relax and rely on them. Probably too much.

They were expert hunters as well – completely silent as they waited for their prey and then pounced. One of them could do that while the rest of us travelled on, and then they'd magically reappear as we lit a fire for supper. Bramble too would do a bit of airflitting, and come back from some store goodness knows where with a bag of cobnuts or some other goodies.

I was surprised how much we were able to keep to woodland, and thoughts of Normans gradually started to fade. It seemed like the old England we knew before the invader came. It felt like home.

On the second evening we were together, Mugwort cleared his throat and said, almost shyly, "Um, I were wonderin', Wulf, if I couldn' have another look at that there rune o' your'n?"

"Of course," I said, and drew it out from under my shirt. "You can hold it if you like. It doesn't let anyone else hold it unless its owner says so, and I seem to be its owner at the moment. Though I know it's only on loan," I added.

I pulled the leather thong over my head and gave it to Mugwort. His eyes shone as he cradled the stone in one hand and traced the etched rune shape with his finger.

"Amazin' things, them runes," he whispered. "'Tis a mystery to me why Pooka be so agin them."

I remembered Pooka well, and how he didn't approve of the runes. He was the chief of their elf clan, although they never did anything without holding a council and voting.

"I s'pose," said Mugwort even more hesitantly, "I s'pose I couldn't see the others? The ones what you got from ol' Gethin's castle?"

We'd told the elves about our recent adventures, the spell-ridden castle and the dragon ride.

"Oz!" I called. "Bring the runes over. Mugwort wants to have a look."

Oz was deep in conversation with Hild, which he seemed to be a lot nowadays, but he cheerfully broke off and dug in his bag for the leather purse containing the rune-stones. He shook it out and Mugwort's face was a picture of wonder.

"An' you reckons these was made by ol' One-eye hisself?"

We nodded and he just sat and gazed at them.

"Be careful," said Bron nervously. "I don't think you should leave them out too long."

"You can feel their power," whispered Hild in awe.

"D'you want to have a go at reading them?" suggested Oz.

Hild shook her head. "I wouldn't dare. Bron's right, they should be put away."

"Thistle got a rune," said Bramble suddenly. "Ain't you, my love?"

Thistle nodded shyly, though she was getting used to us. She pulled something out from inside her dress and showed it to us proudly. Round her neck, on its own little leather thong, was a wooden disc with a rune etched on to it.

Thorn. My own rune.

"I give it to her on her name day," said Mugwort. "Ol' Pooka kicked up a fuss, but I said as how 'twere a 'th' for Thistle. An' 'tis true, you can use the runes for writin'."

"He still didn' like it, tho', ol' Pooka, did he?" grinned Toadstool.

"But I were determined," said Mugwort. "'Twere the best thing I could think of to give her, for protection and to be special to her."

"Yous got to understand, you humans," explained Toadstool, "that it be a right rare thing for an elf baby to be born. So 'twere a cause o' great rejoicin' when Bramble here had this little one."

Bramble nodded proudly.

"And 'tis usual that the baby be one of us reborn. Some elf what's met an untimely death."

What? They were losing me.

"An' we knowed, Toadstool an' me," put in Bramble, "that our baby were my sister Thistle come back to us."

What? I looked around at the others and saw wide eyes and gaping mouths.

"Hang on," said Oz. "Let me get this straight. You reckon your baby is actually Bramble's sister as well as her daughter?"

"'Tis true," nodded Toadstool. "Though o' course, she be a bit different. She be her own little person as well."

I looked at him in disbelief. What spooked me, if this were true, was that Toadstool had loved Thistle in one way, but now he loved her in quite a different way, as his daughter. I shook my head. Suddenly the elves seemed completely alien to me. I couldn't get my head round it. To be honest, it seemed a bit, well...yuck.

When you were living alongside elves they seemed like little humans, almost like children, with their small size and lack of beards, but this reminded me that they were ancient, as old as the land and utterly different from us.

"I 'specks that do seem strange to you," said Mugwort, and we all nodded. He settled himself down and tried to explain.

"We hears as how humans do believe you goes somewheres else when you dies. Some heaven or hell that I doesn't know nothin' about. But we doesn't need nothin' like that. This here land be our home, these woods an' these moors. Who could want nothin' else? An' we lives a long, long time, much longer 'n yous all could imagine. So when the end *do* come, what be better 'n for your spirit to come back to these same woods an' moors, an' back to the elves you already knowed? An' thass what happened to Thistle here."

"An' right glad we be to have her back," said Bramble, giving her child a hug.

Put like that it made sense and it made the world seem bigger and stranger, but in a good way.

"You better put these here stones away, as the maids did say," said Mugwort then. "Anyways, 'tis time to sleep."

"Oh, wait a minute," said Hild. "Let me have one more look."

She spread the stones out lovingly, fingering each one as if it were a precious jewel, before putting them back in their bag and giving them to Oz.

"You know," she said. "I thought I was coming on this quest to help you. I thought I'd be reading my rune-staves and telling you what to do next." She smiled and shook her head. "But all I've done so far is had my mind opened so wide I'm not sure there's room left in it for anything else. What with Woden's ravens and living with you elves...I never thought I'd see such wonders."

"And you haven't met a dragon yet!" said Oz.

"Not sure I want to!" laughed Hild.

The next day Bramble said goodbye to us, but before she left she put her head on one side and looked me in the eye.

"We was wondrin', Wulf, if you seed a green mound on your way to these here woods."

A tingle ran up and down my spine.

"Yes, I did," I nodded.

"Yous can visit that if you gets the chance," she said. "'Cos that's your mother's grave."

"What?" exclaimed Oz. "How did that happen?"

But I knew. "Oh, thank you," I gasped. "Thank you so much. We didn't have time, we were in such a rush to escape the Normans."

"We knowed that," said Toadstool. "An' besides, us elves do that kind o' thing better'n yous could."

"There'll be flowers growin' on it in the spring," put in Mugwort.

"And I thought we'd be able to come back and bury her properly," I went on. "But we've never had the time."

"We knows that an' all," said Bramble. "So yous don' have to worry about it no more."

I thought of my mum lying there peacefully now, no doubt with some elf magic to keep her safe, and I was filled with love for our friends. I wanted to say something else but I choked up. Bronwen said it for me.

"We'll never forget you and your kindness," and she bent and kissed Bramble. Then little Thistle held up her face for a kiss, so she got one too. And the two of them vanished, air-flitting to who knows where.

The day after that Toadstool and Mugwort bade farewell too.

"We've had a good look," said Toadstool, "and there ain't none o' them foreign humans in this part o' the wood. But when you gets to the end o' the wood you best be right careful, as I be sure you knows. Grimwold's place ain't far now, an' you bin here before, so 'taint completely strange to you."

Then Hild said something that I'd thought of but would never have asked myself.

"I don't like to ask this," she started, "as you've already been so good to us, but I was wondering if you couldn't airflit in, grab the stones and come back."

The two elves stiffened and I wished she hadn't said anything.

"We won't take no umbrage," said Mugwort, though it was obvious that they had a bit, "'cause you doesn't understand what you be askin', but we can't risk doin' that. Toadstool here got to get safe back to Bramble an' Thistle as he did promise them, but I couldn't do it neither."

"Yous must all understand," said Toadstool, "that that there Grimwold were a powerful magician. Not quite so much as Gethin, but powerful enough. He'll have put spells round where them runes be hidden, and his spells be right strong. They was strong enough to stop my Thistle escapin' and we can't be riskin' that.

"We wishes you well, but it ain't our adventure. Whatever do happen to you humans, the land'll still be here an' the elves'll still be here."

Mugwort nodded. "'Tis up to all yous now."

"Yes, thank you, thank you," I said.

"We're so grateful for what you've done," said Bron.

"And I'm sorry I asked," said Hild, blushing. "You're right, I didn't really understand."

"Thass a'right," nodded Mugwort. "Don' take it to heart. Goodbye now, and good luck."

There was a shift in the air, and where the elves had been was just earth and grass.

Oz put his arm round Hild, who looked crestfallen, and we turned our faces in the direction of Grimwold's hall.

It wasn't far to the edge of the forest, and when we got there my heart plummeted to my boots. The estate was on the outskirts of a small township, but we were on the side away from the town and had a good view. A lot of it was a burnt-out wreck, thanks to the elf-fire they'd started when they rescued us. And there wasn't an English person in sight, so we wouldn't have to worry about Grimwold's men.

But the place was teeming with Norman soldiers.

CHAPTER THIRTY-THREE

"Oh, great!" Oz shook his head. "This is gonna be dead easy."

We stood just inside the forest, peering through the bare tree branches, and we stared. No-one else could think of anything to say. I couldn't see how we could possibly get into Grimwold's hall and find the rune-stones. We'd have an arrow in us as soon as anyone noticed us.

Then I realized I was wrong about not seeing anyone English. True there were no English soldiers, none of Grimwold's men, but there *were* people working in the fields. Downtrodden people who weren't Norman. The day was overcast and chill and these English workers looked as dejected as the weather. Their backs were bent and they were moving slowly, until a soldier yelled at them, or shoved them.

And then I started to get angry. Angry with the Normans for all they were doing to our homeland.

And angry with Woden. He just loved giving us impossible things to do. I felt like chucking his stones up in the air, saying, 'Here you are – catch!' and walking away.

"Let's get well out of sight," suggested Bronwen, "and think up some sort of plan."

We retreated a little way and found somewhere we could all sit, because it was stupid standing where they might see us. But I didn't reckon anyone was going to come up with a plan.

"One step at a time," said Hild. "This is where my rune-staves come in."

What was it with these girls? They didn't give up easily, that's for sure. And then I began to feel a bit ashamed of myself, because that's exactly what I was doing.

"Not being funny," said Oz, "but I don't think your rune-staves are gonna help us do the impossible."

Hild gave him a withering glare.

"Please give her a chance," said Bron. "I don't think you've got a better idea, have you?"

"All right, all right," muttered Oz.

"Fine," said Hild grumpily. "I need quiet. Nobody say anything. I have to ask a question, then try to interpret what they tell me. And they always *do* tell me something useful."

I shrugged. She might as well have a go, though I was expecting a big fat nothing. We settled ourselves on the ground and Hild got out her little bag of wooden staves. Then she bowed her head and sat in silence for a bit. We all watched her intently.

Suddenly she dipped into the bag and threw a few staves on the ground.

"We need to get into Grimwold's Hall, find Woden's rune-stones and get out again safely," she said, not to us, but to the runes. "Please tell us how to do it."

Then she gently touched each stave in turn without disturbing its position. Now it had started Oz looked completely gripped, as he had when my mum used to consult her runes. I was being drawn in too, and by the look on her face so was Bron.

We sat in silence for some time before Hild said, "I don't understand. They're saying we don't have to find a way, or something like that."

"Do they mean we can give up and go home?" I asked. Perhaps my instinct had been right after all. Perhaps I wasn't such a coward. Let Woden find his own rune-stones!

"No," said Hild. "It's more like, the way will become clear. It'll be shown to us...or something." She frowned. "I've never had a message quite like this."

Bron put her hand on Hild's arm.

"Sometimes, when I've had a vision," she said, "the meaning isn't at all obvious to me. Sometimes I just have to wait until it becomes clear."

"Well, it's never happened to me before," said Hild, and her frown deepened.

"I know!" said Oz brightly. "The ravens are going to turn up and show us a secret path to wherever the runes are."

"You wish!" I retorted. "So we just have to sit and wait for them? And where are the runes, anyway, Bron? I mean, I know they're in Grimwold's place, but where exactly?"

"Well, at the back of the great feasting hall are three separate rooms. I mean proper rooms with doors, with keys. It's an amazing place," she said. "Not like Gethin's castle, of course, but far bigger and more complicated than most halls."

"And the runes are in one of these rooms?" asked Oz.

"Yes. Abdul and I were kept in the two on the right, next to each other. We could talk to each other through a door in the wall, though unfortunately that was locked, like the doors to our rooms. And on the far left was a third room and in my vision I went in and saw there was a door in the floor. I opened it and it led down some wooden steps to an underground chamber. That's where the rune-stones are."

"You saw all that when you only blacked out for a few heartbeats?" said Oz incredulously.

"Oz!" I warned him.

I didn't want Bron losing her temper with him as she had in the past. But I needn't have worried.

She just smiled. "Yes, Osric," she said, as if she were talking to a child. "I saw all that in that short time."

"Sorry," grinned Oz. "I wasn't really disbelieving you."

"I thought you said the place was all burnt down," said Hild.

"Most of it was," I said, "but perhaps the hall itself wasn't as badly damaged as the rest."

"It had painted wooden tiles on the roof," said Bron. "Of course, wood burns, but not as quickly as the straw thatch on the other buildings. Perhaps they concentrated on putting the fire out in the main hall. That would be the most valuable place. It had lovely wall-hangings, and carved dragons either side of the entrance. I'm sure they'd try to protect that first."

I suddenly had a bright idea.

"Look," I said, "why don't *we* pretend to be working in the fields like that lot? We'd have to hide our weapons, of course."

"How could we do that?" Oz objected. "Hide them somewhere they couldn't be seen but would be easy for us to grab when we needed them? That's tricky."

"And I'd have to pretend to be English," said Bron, "so I'd better not say anything. I don't suppose there's anyone with a Welsh accent out there."

"You could say you'd been a servant," said Hild, "which is absolutely true. But anyway, I'm going to hide my rune-staves in my dress. I won't be parted from *them*."

"Yeah, good idea," said Oz, producing the little bag with Woden's runes in. "I'm putting these inside my tunic."

We were all talking at once now, which was why we weren't paying proper attention. And that made it easy for the group of Normans who jumped us. As rough arms grabbed us from behind and sword points found our throats, I cursed our stupidity. We knew the Normans were near! Why hadn't we been more careful? Or...was this meant to be?

So Bron was right. The meaning of the runes' message did become clear. At least the first bit, about getting there. But unfortunately Oz was wrong. As we were overpowered, there was no sign at all of Woden's ravens.

CHAPTER THIRTY-FOUR

I automatically tried to draw my sword but one of the Normans wrenched my arm away and we were soon having our hands tied behind our backs. The soldiers were none too gentle and my wrists burned from the tight ropes. It hurt less if you didn't struggle. Oz had been hiding Woden's runes inside his tunic, so he hadn't had a chance even to try and grab a weapon. But that was all right. I think we knew that in some mysterious way this was meant to happen. It was how we were going to reach Grimwold's place without getting an arrow in us.

The group leader looked us up and down.

"My captain 'as decided to use zis place as a base," he said in heavily accented English, "but it needs rebuilding. You two boys will work at zat, while ze girls can cook and serve ze men. If you are useful we might not kill you."

I looked at Bron and Hild, and sincerely hoped they were only going to be serving food and not themselves. Hild had made a face when he talked about cooking, but she was too sensible to say anything.

They took all our weapons – swords, knives and bows and arrows – and marched us across the fields towards Grimwold's hall. It went against all my instincts not to put up a bit of a fight or try to make a break for it (although both would have been suicidal) but those soldiers were taking us exactly where we wanted to go. Hild's puzzling rune reading seemed to be playing out. Quite what we'd be able to do without a single weapon, I wasn't sure.

When I got the chance I mouthed to Oz, "Got the runes?" and he gave a slight nod of his head. It was hard walking across the uneven ground with our arms tied behind our backs, so we stumbled a lot. You don't think how much you use your arms when you walk – until you can't use them.

Soon we started to pass other captured English people digging around in the ground. What were they doing? I was about to ask one, but as soon as I opened my mouth I got a hard shove which made me stagger and almost fall. Most of the crops had been burnt as far as I could see, and it was way too early to be sowing new ones. Then I saw an old man pull a mangy looking parsnip up out of the blackened earth and I understood. They were grubbing about for whatever root vegetables they could find. The roots didn't look great. They must have been affected by having their green tops burnt, even though the roots themselves were underground. And the miserable looking workers weren't doing it to feed themselves. A Norman soldier was wandering around, shouting at anyone he didn't think was putting his back into it.

Oz raised an eyebrow.

"That's clever!" he said. "You burn the crops and then..."

He didn't get a chance to finish before he was sprawled face down in the mud. Of course, he couldn't save himself, so when he was kicked into a kneeling position his face was covered in mud and one cheek was bleeding. He must have fallen on to a stone. The soldier who had kicked him grabbed his arm and dragged him up.

"Please do not try anyssing else," said the one in charge – he seemed to be the only one who spoke English. "I 'ave not much patience."

I frowned at Oz in what I hoped was a warning way. Idiot! He just couldn't keep his big mouth shut. The last thing we wanted was one of us dead, or even with a broken arm or leg. The girls were looking at him all sympathetic, but I just hoped he'd learnt to shut up. Which he seemed to have done, because the rest of the forced march went smoothly enough.

When we got there I wondered why they were bothering to repair the place. All the outbuildings were completely burnt down. One thing about the Normans, they could throw up a wooden fortress in no time at all. Why not just leave this and build one of their own? But then we were separated from the girls and me and Oz were shoved in the direction of Grimwold's actual hall.

And I saw what Bron meant. It was enormous and still magnificent, even with the roof gone. Of course, not like Gethin's castle, but *that* was in a class all of its own. I mean, as far as English great halls go, this was really something. I reckoned Bron was right. They must have concentrated their efforts and all their buckets of water on this place. There was even part of an incredible wall hanging left, which looked like the World Ash Tree in our stories. We shook our heads in wonder.

"You two will work on ze roof," said our friendly overseer. "We 'ave been chopping down trees, so it can just be made of timber. 'Ere, Guilbert, zese two are for you."

And he prodded us over to a burly man directing things from below. Guilbert also spoke some English, of a sort, and he was just as matey as the one who'd captured us. He cut through our ropes with a knife, nicking my hand in the process, and took us to a rickety looking ladder.

"Nails," he said, handing us each a little bag. "'Ammer," though it was more of a wooden mallet. "Zey put ze plank in place and you nail it. If you fall you break your neck. Now go!"

I followed Oz up the ladder and at last we found some people we could talk to. Two young men a bit older than us were manoeuvring a long plank into place at the bottom of the roof. They nodded at us with rueful smiles on their faces. It was as if they were saying, *we know we ought to be fighting the bastards, but what can you do?*

"I'm Alf and this is Beocca," said one.

"Wulf," and, "Oz", we muttered back.

"It'll be easier with you two," said Alf.

"Easier?" said Beocca. "It's practically impossible with just the two of us. We heard what happy Harold said about breaking your necks and he wasn't kidding."

"It's my first day up here," said Alf, "replacing Cerdic who *did* fall and break his neck."

"Great," said Oz. "Sounds like we'd be better off back in the army."

"Oz got badly wounded," I explained, "so we got left behind."

"I've got a gammy leg now, so I wasn't much use for fighting any more," said Beocca. "It makes it difficult up here, but it does make me extra careful."

"And I just got jumped," said Alf. "We were a small group and there were loads of them. They decided to put us to work instead of killing us."

So we'd all been fighting in the resistance and we'd all ended up working for the enemy. Slaves, in fact.

"But we'll get our own back," muttered Beocca darkly. "One day."

"What are you doing up zere?" came a shout from below.

"All right, you get the idea," said Beocca loudly, pointing to the planks. "They've put the frames up and these planks are more or less shaped, though you'll get a load of splinters in your hands. We fix this one to the bottom, then the next one'll overlap a bit, and so on to the top."

There were quite long spaces between the wooden triangles that formed the shape of the roof, so you really did need more than two workers. Alf and Beocca held the plank in place at each end and me and Oz nailed it in. But you had to keep your balance at the same time. It would be very easy to slip and it was a long way down.

We didn't get a chance to talk privately as Oz was at one end of the plank and I was at the other, concentrating like mad on not falling. But I *was* having a good look at what was below us. We were at one end of the hall and I was trying to work out whether this was the end with the three rooms that Bron had talked about. It was such a mess down there that it was hard to see, but I thought it was. It looked as though the remains of internal walls were still there, though mostly burnt.

When we finally reached the top we were gasping for something to drink and Guilbert, or Happy Harold, as Beocca called him, told us to come down. We were given some dry bread by a miserable looking English girl, and some very weak watered ale.

"God, I hope the girls are all right," muttered Oz.

I gulped down some ale and nodded.

"Oz," I whispered, "I think we might be working right above the place we're looking for."

"Yeah, I thought so too."

"We'll just have to hope these Normans sleep somewhere else. We can't do a thing in the daytime."

"Or we'll have to be super quiet and careful at stepping over sleeping bodies," said Oz.

"I was wondering if we ought to try and do it without the girls," I suggested. "It's bound to be dangerous, and if we manage we can always find them afterwards."

Oz shook his head. "We need Bron. She'll know exactly where the place is, and we could waste a lot of time looking for it. The quicker we are, the safer it'll be."

"I suppose so," I muttered, "though you *could* say there's more to go wrong with four of us."

But Oz was determined. "We've got to find the girls first. Hild'll kill me if she misses out on the action."

"Oh, so that's what it's about!" I said.

"No, I really think we need Bron," said Oz.

"Enough talking," barked Guilbert. "Get up zere and start working!"

As we climbed the ladder I thought of all the steps we had to take to find Woden's precious runes.

Wait till everyone's asleep. Find the girls. Creep around all the sleeping Normans. Find the door in the floor. Open it and go down. Find the runes. Come back up and, somehow, escape.

Dead easy.

CHAPTER THIRTY-FIVE

Later on, tired and sweaty despite the autumn chill, we sat eating more dry bread and waiting for some of that delicious weak ale. Gnat's piddle, Oz called it. We both smiled when we saw who was walking round with the jug. We'd been given a leather cup and had to keep that on us, to be filled when our overlords reckoned we'd done enough work to deserve a drink.

"Are you and Hild all right?" I whispered to Bron as she bent over us pouring the ale.

"Yes, don't worry," she whispered back, "though I wouldn't want to stay here too long."

"We think we know where they are," muttered Oz. "The runes, I mean. Shall we give it a go tonight?"

She shook her head. "We both think it should be tomorrow night. Hild managed to duck behind a wall and do a quick reading, and the runes said tomorrow. I must say I feel the same thing."

Oz looked at me and shrugged.

"I just want to get it over," he said.

"We must wait for the conditions to be right," whispered Bron. "What you call the web of Wyrd, all the invisible threads that connect everything. We think that's tomorrow night."

"Come on, hurry up with that ale!" yelled someone, and Bron had to move on.

But first she bent and whispered in my ear, "Wait for me round the corner. Over there." She jerked her head in the direction of the cooking area. Just you."

I nodded and gulped down some ale. A mouth-watering aroma was wafting over to us as we sat there, still hungry.

"God, that smells good!" sighed Oz. "Wonder if we ever get any of that, or do the English have to survive on dry bread?"

A deer was roasting on a spit and soldiers were gathering round, joking and laughing, waiting for their share of the feast. An English boy about our age was turning the spit and another was basting the meat with fat dripping into a ladle he was holding underneath.

"I hope *they* get some at any rate, though I doubt *we'll* get any tonight," I said.

"That's good of you," muttered Oz. "I don't care about them, I just want some myself."

"Well, imagine being that close and having that smell right under your nose and then not getting any!"

"I suppose," agreed Oz.

"Anyway, Bron wants a private word," I said. "D'you think they'll mind if I wander round?"

In fact, people were getting up and stretching, gathering into little groups and talking to each other. There were guards keeping an eye on things, but it seemed they didn't mind us moving so long as no-one tried to escape. The day's work seemed to be over as the dusk deepened. It would be hard to see properly what you were doing, even with the almost full moon sailing up into the sky.

"I'm going to go and find Hild," said Oz, slurping down the last of his ale.

I headed in the direction Bron had indicated, and there she was, waiting for me.

"Come over here," she smiled. "We may not be undisturbed for long, and there's something I want to give you."

She took my hand and pulled me towards the ruins of a little stone building. It must once have been a church, although from what I knew of Grimwold he wouldn't have spent much time in it. Churches were practically the only buildings made of stone, which was one of the things that made Gethin's castle so amazing. I looked around for Norman guards and caught the eye of one lounging nearby. He shrugged and winked at me. It was obvious what he thought we were doing.

Bron pulled me into a sort of alcove, a corner between two ruined bits of wall. It wasn't quite dark, with the light of the cooking fires flickering though gaps in the wall and the brilliant moon overhead, but it was private. I didn't say anything. What could she be going to give me?

"Wulf, what we're going to do with the runes is very dangerous," she began.

"I know that," I whispered, "and that's why I've been thinking me and Oz should do this on our own."

"No!" she said firmly. "We're all in this together. But the thing is, we may not all live."

She hadn't let go of my hand and now I pulled her towards me.

"*You're* going to live, whatever happens!" I said fiercely. "I won't let you get hurt!"

"Don't be silly, Wulf. You may not be able to stop it. Of course we're all going to do our best to stay alive, but...just in case..."

She pulled her hand away and started fiddling with something inside her overdress. Finally she brought out a little cloth bag and tipped its contents into one hand.

It was a necklace. A beautiful necklace made of different colour stones.

"It's the most precious thing I have, or am ever likely to have," she whispered. "Lady Rhiannon gave it to me when I left her service."

"It's beautiful," I whispered back. "What's it made of?"

"It's called amber," said Bron, "from the country of the northmen."

"Move into the light," I said, "so I can see the colours properly."

We shifted into a little pool of firelight flickering through a gap in the wall and she held it up for me. As it swung in the warm glow of the fire I could see its colours almost as if it were day. Dark brown, light brown and shades of green. I watched the necklace swinging gently and then I looked at Bron's face, lit by the same flickering glow. A slight smile played on her lips and her eyes had a far away look, as if she were remembering something.

"Your eyes," I said.

"What about them?" she asked.

I felt sorry because I'd disturbed her memories, but I wanted to say this.

"Your eyes are the same colour as the amber, at least in this light. They're brown and gold and green, all mixed together."

She smiled. "Lady Rhiannon said the same thing when she gave it to me. She said it was to thank me for my service and she said…never mind."

"What? What did she say?"

"It doesn't matter, Wulf."

"No, I want to know what she said."

"Well, all right. She said…she said I was to wear it on my wedding day."

I pulled her closer to me and something gave me the courage to say what I'd been longing to say, but never thought I'd dare.

"You must!" I whispered. "You must wear it when you marry *me*!"

She looked startled and for a heartbeat I thought I'd ruined everything. But then she smiled again, her beautiful, gentle smile.

"We'd better make sure, then, that we both stay alive," she whispered back.

I clasped her in both arms and felt my heart soaring up to that moon, the moon that I stupidly felt had given me the courage to say it. I knew it was ridiculous but that's what I felt. Her body felt so slight in my arms and I wanted to protect her from all the danger we were in, wanted never to let her go. But as I kissed the top of her head she gently pushed me away. She was still smiling though, almost laughing, and I couldn't believe what had just happened.

"Are you…?" I stuttered. "I mean, are you actually saying that you'll marry me?"

"Yes, of course," she said. "I've always liked you. I mean, liked you… like that…even when we were on Lord Aelfric's estate. But since we met again it's grown."

"Well, I wish you'd given me a little hint," I said.

"But you must have known I felt differently about you from the way I felt about Osric."

"Yeah, obviously! Because you two were always at each other's throats!"

Now she really laughed. "Well, now you know. But Wulf, we don't have long and I haven't said what I wanted to."

Oh yes, I'd forgotten. She wanted to give me something.

"Just in case I don't live, I want you to have something to remember me by."

"No!" I said. "That's not going to happen. There's no way you're going to die and I'm going to live!"

"Don't argue!" she said. "We haven't got long. I want you to have this necklace as a keepsake."

She opened one of my hands and let it drop into the palm. I frowned. I didn't like the way this conversation had turned. But then I brightened up.

"All right," I said. "I'll keep it for you until our wedding day. I don't suppose I'll have much else to give you, so I'll fasten it round your neck as a wedding gift."

"Done!" she grinned.

But then I had an even better idea.

"And I've got something to give *you*," I said, and pulled my leather thong over my head. The rune Thorn swung in the firelight and I thought I could feel its power. Could feel it speaking to me, consenting to what I was doing. "This is more of a loan, because if we manage to get the rest of Woden's runes I'm sure he'll want this one back as well. But it will help keep you safe meanwhile."

Bron gazed at it wide-eyed.

"But Wulf, this really *is* precious," she said.

Then she bowed her head so I could put it round her neck.

"Remember," I told her. "You hold it up in front of your enemy and say, 'By the power of Thorn I command you to stop'."

She nodded, then thrust the bag with the necklace into my hand and I hid it inside my shirt. Just in time too. The soldier who'd winked at me came round the corner and gestured that it was time for us to go back to the others. I think he was disappointed to find us both fully clothed and apparently having a chat.

As we came out of the church I saw Oz with his arm round Hild, both of them laughing and looking pleased with themselves.

The next day Oz and me were both in a ridiculously good mood considering our circumstances. I was even enjoying the feel of the wood under my hand (despite the splinters) and the power of the hammer knocking the nails in.

"It won't last though, this roof," said Beocca.

"Why not?" I asked, but then realized I knew the answer. "Oh, because it hasn't been seasoned."

"That's right," said Beocca. "They've only just cut the trees down. It'll warp."

I suddenly had a picture of myself, when all this was over, cutting wood and storing it to season, building things, having a life. It was the first time I could remember feeling good about the future. Even *thinking* about the future, apart from wondering when the next battle was going to be. Of course, there were the Normans. Perhaps me and Bron would go and live in Wales. I'd have to learn Welsh!

As the day drew to a close the moon appeared in the sky and everyone gasped. It was full now and looked huge, but that wasn't why people were gasping. It was an orange moon, almost red. There were mutters about what it meant. Was it a good omen or a bad? A blood moon, they were calling it.

"I've just realized something," said Oz, as we settled down to our inevitable bread and wishy-washy ale.

I raised my eyebrows.

"Well, we've all lost track of time but it must be November by now."

"And?" I mumbled through a mouthful of dry bread.

"Don't you remember what the old name for November was?"

Of course!

"Blood Month!" I spluttered, spraying crumbs everywhere.

"Exactly! And this is a blood moon! The first full moon in Blood Month!"

I managed to swallow. "Do you reckon this is part of what the girls were talking about? About everything being in alignment?"

"Yeah, I'm sure it is!" said Oz. "So we'd better eat quickly and get ready."

Looking up at that huge blood moon glowering down at us, I didn't share Oz's confidence. It didn't look like a good omen to me.

When Oz said *get ready*, he didn't mean we had any weapons to collect. We had nothing apart from our hammers, and they were back by the ladder. We didn't even have any grand plans. We just had to keep our eyes and ears open, keep an eye on where the girls were, and wait for people to start dozing off. Then we had to take the first opportunity we could.

But as things started to quieten down a bit and English and Normans settled for the night, there was the sound of horses' hooves. The horses stopped. We could hear people dismounting, and then voices. Voices talking in English but not with English accents. One of the voices had a heavy Norman accent. That was Guilbert, our overseer. The other spoke English much better but with a slight lilt.

Oz gripped my arm and my blood froze.

We knew that voice.

CHAPTER THIRTY-SIX

"Madoc!" breathed Oz.

"So much for waiting for the conditions to be right," I muttered.

"We could have done it last night and been away from here," said Oz through gritted teeth.

"Sh!" I hushed him. "Listen!"

Their voices had risen and there seemed to be an argument developing.

"But we will not disturb you," Madoc was saying. "We are not your enemies, we are Welsh."

"I shall 'ave to fetch ze camp commander," said Guilbert gruffly.

But he didn't have to fetch him, as the commander was striding over. And behind him, keeping close to the walls, crept two shadows. Hild and Bron. Me and Oz looked at each other and casually stood up and stretched.

"Let's find a place to sleep," yawned Oz.

"I dropped my hammer into the hall," I said. "I'd better go and find it."

"I'll come with you," said Oz.

We sauntered towards a gap in the wall that led into the main hall. It was madness, of course, but what else could we do? When I'd first heard Madoc's voice the thought had flashed through my mind that we might as well give up. But that was it, just a flash. Then something else took over. We'd come this far – we weren't going to give up now! The look of grim determination on Oz's face told me that he felt the same.

Madoc was obviously trying to keep his temper and not create trouble.

"The English lord of this hall stole something valuable that belonged to my lord, a noble Welshman."

"What 'as zat to do wiz us?" growled the commander.

"We only want to retrieve it," went on Madoc, "to return it to its rightful owner."

"But ze 'all is ours now. If zis sing is valuable it should belong to us."

That's it, keep him talking, I thought desperately. It was so hard to saunter when we wanted to run.

"It is purely of sentimental value," Madoc was saying. "It would be of no interest to you."

Finally we reached the gap and shot inside.

"Careful!" muttered Oz, for there were some bodies bedding down for the night, both English and Norman.

It was almost as light inside the hall as out for there wasn't much roof built, and that moon was still glowering down. Watching us, I felt. But there were plenty of shadows round the walls and in corners so we kept to these because we didn't want to be noticed. That had its own dangers though.

"Ouch! Careful, you clodhopper!" growled a voice as I nearly tripped over someone.

"Sorry," I muttered. "Just trying to find somewhere to sleep."

"There's plenty of room without kicking me," grumbled the voice.

"Sorry," I said again, but then I was startled by another voice, a deep voice that I'd heard before, but that didn't belong to Oz.

Hurry, it said. *Keep going. Your friends are already there.*

I mean, it didn't sound like Oz, and Oz wouldn't say *your friends*, but I couldn't think who else it could be.

"What did you say?" I asked him.

"Nothing, but we'd better get a move on."

Osric is right, said the voice and I stopped stock still.

It was right inside my head, that voice, not coming through my ears at all. I remembered something like this once before when I'd travelled back in time with Gethin and I met the god Cernunnos. That's how he'd talked to me. That's one of the ways gods could talk to you. And I knew then who it was.

"Woden," I breathed.

"What?" muttered Oz. "Come on, what's the matter with you? I can see the girls already in the chamber. How did they get there so quickly?"

Hurry, said Woden in my head. *Bronwen will show you the way.*

I stumbled after Oz not sure how I put one foot in front of the other. There was no-one trying to sleep in that little chamber behind the main hall, probably because it was such a mess of boulders and burnt wood. It had been separated from the hall by a wall and a door, but only part of the wall was now left standing.

"I've found the entrance we need," whispered Bron, "but we have to clear stuff away from it."

And there it was, a square door but in the floor instead of a wall. I'd never seen such a thing.

"That's weird," said Hild. "A door in the floor."

"I think it's called a trapdoor," said Bron, though I didn't know how she knew that. Perhaps they'd had one in Lord Aelfric's hall.

"Yeah," muttered Oz, "because once you're down there you're trapped."

As quickly and quietly as we could, we shifted the rubble away and then saw a bolt and an iron ring.

Oz tugged at the rusting bolt. It was stiff and creaky, but he managed, and then we both grabbed the big iron ring and heaved up the heavy wooden door.

It was pitch black down there.

"We need a torch," gasped Hild, "and there's no time now to get one!"

We wouldn't have brought one even if we'd had time, though, because we didn't want to be seen. Then the voice spoke again.

Quickly! said Woden. *Tell Osric to get out the runes!*

"Um, Oz," I muttered. "Get the runes out."

"What?" said Oz. "Now? What for?"

"Just do it and I'll tell you in a minute."

In the half light I could see Oz roll his eyes in disbelief, but he reached inside his shirt and fished out the little bag with Woden's runes in.

"Ouch, it's getting hot!" he said.

"And so is mine!" gasped Bron pulling Thorn out from her dress.

Oz and Hild gaped, partly because they didn't know I'd given it to her, but mainly because it was glowing brightly.

Oz opened the drawstring of his bag and a golden light lit his face and hands.

"Woden's given us torches", I grinned. Hey, perhaps it was going to be all right! The god hadn't always given us the help we needed, but it seemed he was doing his bit now.

Suddenly there were footsteps and voices coming our way.

Get down there! said Woden urgently inside my head, but we'd all had the same thought.

There was a wooden ladder, lit now by the light of the runes, and we scrambled down on to a rough earth floor, Hild first, then Bron, then me and lastly Oz. It smelt musty and dank down there and the chill from the ground seeped right up through the soles of my boots. Oz stayed on the ladder and struggled to bring the door down, and I stood one rung below him to help.

On the inside was another bolt. Whoever had had this built, presumably Grimwold, had obviously not wanted to be disturbed. I shuddered as I wondered what had gone on in this place.

Lock the door, said Woden, and I repeated his instructions.

Oz gave me a funny look, but he slid the bolt across.

Just in time, as the voices came right overhead. We could hear someone tugging at the ring and then Madoc's voice.

"It is locked on the inside," he said. "Someone is down there and I think I know who it is." Then in an echo of Oz's words, "Never mind. They are trapped!"

CHAPTER THIRTY-SEVEN

From that point on, rather than panicking I felt that time slowed. We were down there, probably with no way out and enemies waiting for us just above our heads. A hopeless situation. But hearing Woden's voice and seeing the glowing runes had shifted my mood. We'd been sent here by a god and I felt now that he wasn't going to let us down.

"Right," said Hild in a tight voice, "let's find the other runes and see if there's another way out."

"How big is this place?" asked Oz, holding up his open bag of runes.

The golden glow lit up the ceiling – just wooden planks, the underside of the floor up above. Bronwen too held up her little light, the rune-stone Thorn that I'd given her. She started to walk away from the trapdoor, following the earthen wall, and Oz did the same on the other side of the underground chamber.

"Look!" said Hild, "What's in that?"

A little further along stood a wooden chest. An ornately carved chest, which surely held more than clothes. We crowded round it and I tried to lift the lid. It wouldn't budge, so Oz joined in.

"That's no good, it's locked," said Bronwen, as we heaved at it. "There's a keyhole, but no key."

"Are there any shelves where you could put a key?" I suggested, but a quick sweep of the rune bag round the chamber revealed completely bare earth walls.

There was a loud banging on the trapdoor, but we ignored it. Hild crouched down and started to run her hands over the damp ground.

"Shine a light down here, will you?" she said impatiently. "And spread out. We'll have to try and search the whole floor. There must be a key somewhere."

Then the voice came again, echoing in my head. I jumped. It seemed a while since Woden had said anything.

"*Tell Bronwen to hold her rune against the lock*," said the voice.

"Try holding your rune-stone against the lock," I said to Bron, feeling a bit stupid.

"Well, what good's that going to do?" objected Oz.

"Look, I know this sounds really weird. It *is* really weird. But Woden's started talking to me...inside my head, so no-one else can hear. Just do it, Bron."

Oz and Hild gawped at me, but Bron smiled and held her rune up against the lock. There was a click and the lid sprang open.

Suddenly the whole chamber was lit up, as if the runes in the chest were greeting ours, and our runes were saying hello back. It was the most joyful thing we'd seen since...well, for a long, long time. I leaned over into the chest and scooped them up into my hands. There were fewer than we already had and I didn't drop a single one. It was as if those runes wanted to be picked up to join their brothers.

"Tip them on to the ground," said Woden inside my head. "All of them. Thorn as well."

I put mine on the ground and signalled Oz and Bron to do the same.

"You'll have to take it off from round your neck," I said to Bron. "I'm sorry, you haven't had it long."

"No, this is what we've been keeping it for," said Bron, slipping the leather thong over her head.

The banging overhead grew even louder and there was confused shouting too.

We paid it all no mind, because something amazing was happening. The runes slid over the ground, all by themselves, arranging themselves into their groups of eight. They were all there. I started to recite their names, in English of course, the names that Hild and my mum used. But the voice in my head took over and called them names I didn't know. So I repeated the words after Woden. Ancient words, far older than the English language. Woden's original rune names.

Fehu, Uruz, Thurisaz, Ansuz I chanted. *Raidho, Kenaz, Gebo, Wunjo. Hagalaz, Naudhiz, Isa, Jera, Eihwaz, Perthro, Elhaz, Sowilo, Tiwaz, Berkano, Ehwaz, Mannaz, Laguz, Ingwaz, Dagaz, Othala.*

And as I chanted, the runes began to form themselves into a circle, a really big one, with wide spaces in between each rune. They kept to the same order though – three groups of eight. When I stopped, Hild grabbed my arm.

"How did you know those names?" she demanded. "They're not what we usually call them."

"I told you. Woden speaks inside my head. He told me the names to say. I think they're the original names he gave them."

"You mean, like, *Woden*...actual *Woden*...*talks* inside your *head*?" she said, stressing every other word and looking at me as if I'd grown two heads instead of just the one Woden was talking to.

"Well, he's only just started to do that," I admitted. "I told you it was weird."

"Never mind that!" snapped Oz, crouching down and trying to gather up the runes. "We've found them and now we've got to pick them up and find a way out of here."

But the runes didn't want to be picked up.

"Ouch!" hissed Oz, drawing back his hand as if he'd been bitten. "They're too hot! Whose idea was it to chuck them on the ground, anyway?"

"Woden's," I said.

Just then there was an almighty crash above our heads, followed by silence and then Madoc's menacing voice.

"Listen," he said. "I know that you are down there and I know that you have the rune-stones. If you come up now and give them to me, no harm will come to you."

"Yeah, like we believe that," muttered Oz.

"If you do not," Madoc went on, "You will die."

We were all staring up at the trapdoor but a sudden blinding flash of light made us turn back to the circle of runes. Something was forming in the middle of the circle.

Something almost unbearably bright.

Something cross shaped, with a longer upright piece and two slightly shorter arms.

Then as the light gradually dimmed we saw that it was four things arranged in the shape of a cross.

Four beautiful, shining swords. Swords with runic lettering on the blades, spelling out names. Swords often have names, things like *Bonecrusher*, or *Blood-drinker*. But these were not that sort of name. They were *our* names. The swords were named after their rightful owners.

The one at the top had *Wulfstan* inscribed on the blade. Below that was *Osric*. On the left was a shorter sword, a seax, named *Bronwen*. And on the right-hand one, also smaller than the two uprights, was written *Hild*.

In the light of the runes the blades seemed to ripple like water. I don't know what they were made of. I'd never seen anything like it.

The hilts were plain, and we saw now that on the outside of the rune circle were four plain leather scabbards on belts. So if we were walking around with these at our waists, no-one would suspect the incredible beauty of the shining blades. Woden had thought of everything. He knew we weren't like heroes in the old stories, but ordinary people caught up in extraordinary events. And we had to live among ordinary people, not carrying swords with jewelled hilts and scabbards inlaid with gold and silver.

"I am waiting for your answer," came Madoc's voice, but we took no notice.

I walked around the circle and put on my scabbard, while the others did the same. Then we reached in and picked up our swords. I heard the others gasp and I'm sure I did too. For the swords were light and so easy to handle. Mine felt like an extension of my own arm. But better than that, as I tried a few moves I realized that it was doing what I wanted, but far better than I'd ever done before. I'd never wielded a sword so fluently.

I looked at Bron and could scarcely believe how gracefully she was moving, how different she seemed from the clumsy novice that Hild had been coaching. Her amazed expression showed that she too was finding it hard to believe. Hild's face shone with joy and Oz was grinning his head off.

"Thank you, Woden," I whispered. "Thank you."

We almost danced around the circle of runes, practising moves and making circles in the air, until there was an almighty bang. Then we all looked up, swords raised, as an axe blade crashed through the trapdoor.

CHAPTER THIRTY-EIGHT

The door splintered and someone tried to pull the axe free, but before he succeeded a second axe split the wood and knocked the bolt from its hinges. We just stood there as, with a mighty creak, the trapdoor was heaved upwards.

"Ah, my little friends," sneered Madoc, and stepped on to the top rung of the ladder.

"Come on then," coaxed Oz. "Come and get us."

Madoc smiled his wolf-like smile and put his other foot on the next rung. Then the next rung.

"Stay back!" he called to his men. "Stay until I command you."

What a cocky fool. Did he think he was going to take all four of us on his own? Then I realized what he was going to do. As he opened his mouth a deep voice began to chant, not Madoc's voice but Gethin's. But before he had finished the first word Oz was on him. He flung himself at Madoc, knocked him off the ladder and put his free hand over the Welshman's mouth. I put my foot on his chest, none too gently, and my sword was at his throat.

Oz yelled and pulled his hand away and the chanting began again, but Hild was there, stuffing the edge of her dress in his mouth. She ripped it off and I bent down and put my sword-free hand over the material, keeping it scrunched up inside his mouth.

"The bugger bit me!" hissed Oz.

Then I heard Bronwen's calm voice. "Stay back if you know what's good for you," she said to the men standing round the trapdoor.

"Idiot girl!" yelled a soldier, and started to come down the ladder. He was shoved from behind and half fell, half jumped, straight on to Bron's upturned seax. She gasped and let go as the moaning body collapsed on to the ground.

"Well done, Bron!" I shouted. "Now get your sword back!"

But before she could recover herself enough to try and pull it out of the soldier's bleeding body, Oz put his foot on the man, grasped the seax and pulled. It came away with a squelch and he wiped it on the soldier's leg and handed it back to Bronwen.

So many things were happening all at once now that there was no time to think, only to react. More soldiers started to climb down the ladder, and Hild darted out of sight behind it. I had to use all my strength to keep Madoc on the ground. I felt we should just kill him but now it came to it, something held me back.

"*What are you waiting for?*" I heard Woden's voice, sounding impatient with me.

Then two other voices yelled and a soldier buckled and fell on top of the one on the rung below. They both collapsed on to the earth floor. The one on top was moaning and crying out and I saw a spout of dark red blood erupting from his leg. Hild darted round from behind the ladder and plunged her seax up under his left arm, finishing him off. She'd been attacking the legs of the descending men and I realized that one of the voices I'd heard was hers, yelling "Woden!" with all her might.

Suddenly, Oz was on the ground as the soldier underneath crawled out from beneath his dead comrade and grabbed Oz's legs. He'd dropped his sword as he fell off the ladder and Bron had kicked it away, but now he was grappling Oz, trying to grab *his* sword. I instinctively went to help and released my hold on Madoc's head but I needn't have worried about helping Oz. That sword didn't want to be wielded by anyone but its master. It turned in Oz's hand and seemed to find its own way into the enemy's stomach, through the mail and the leather, right into his gut. But even as the man gurgled his last breaths another sound filled the underground room. Madoc had spat out the material in his mouth and now a deep and unearthly chanting flowed round us, stopping all movement, all other sounds.

How could I have been so stupid as to let go? All eyes turned to Madoc, still on the ground with my foot on his chest but rippling, changing, his face now Madoc's, now Gethin's, his slim body becoming more powerful until he pushed me off and rose from the floor. Even his own men shrank back horrified and I cursed myself but felt dazed and helpless.

Until Woden took over.

"*Quick, you fool!*" said the voice in my head. "*Before the transformation is complete!*"

Suddenly my mind cleared. This was it. If I couldn't do it now, with this sword that Woden had given me, we were lost. But we weren't going to be lost! I found my strength and plunged that sword into my enemy's midriff. His eyes bulged as we stood facing each other, he taller and more powerful than me. We were joined by a magical sword, the hilt in my hand and the point in his body. A surge of power flowed down my arm, through the blade and into Gethin. Then my body shook as it flowed back towards me. But the sword wasn't having that! It trembled in my hand and the power reversed again and shot into the figure facing me. Then the chanting grew fainter until a gush of blood from Gethin's mouth stopped it all together. His body collapsed on to my weapon and I had to let go as he fell on to the ground and rolled over with the sword sticking out of his front.

The body jerked. It was still Gethin's body but then that strange rippling began again. It was one person then another as everyone stood stock still, staring at it. Until finally it settled and shrank slightly, no longer Gethin but the slim figure of Madoc, lying there dead. Everyone was frozen, gazing at him.

"Poor man," murmured Bron unexpectedly.

Poor man? That's not what I would have called him! But as she went on I understood what she meant.

"At least now that devil won't be able to use his body in that horrible way."

Oz's mouth dropped open, but there was no chance to talk as the soldiers started stirring, blinking as if they'd just woken up.

We were still outnumbered. I put my foot on Madoc's body and pulled my sword out, while the others held theirs at the ready. Bron was standing by the circle of runes, our only source of light. Suddenly a soldier on the ladder roared and leapt at her, pushing her into the middle of the circle. The light grew brighter and brighter and the soldier backed away, leaving Bron on the ground bathed in a golden haze as the runes floated toward the ceiling. She stood up and smiled at them as they rose into the air and then…one blinding lightning flash and they were gone.

Woden had reclaimed his runes.

Our quest was ended. But what about us? Was the god just going to leave us there, facing all these soldiers?

Without the runes' light we were plunged into blackness, but Bron still stood there in a golden glow with tiny sparks flickering over her dress and her long black hair. I thought she looked like an angel, but somebody else had a different idea.

"Look at her!" yelled one of Madoc's men. "Grab her! She's a witch!"

CHAPTER THIRTY-NINE

No! They weren't going to get her! I leapt to her defence but the ground was slick with blood and I slipped. By the time I'd righted myself one of Madoc's men had her by the arm. But not for long. Oz and Hild fell on the man and I joined them. We easily overpowered him, but we were now in the middle of a circle of men chanting in English and Welsh, "Witch, witch! *Gwrach, gwrach*!"

It grew lighter and I realized that our swords had started to glimmer, to make up for the glow from the vanished rune-stones. Then another light blazed out from the top of the ladder as a torch was thrust through the trapdoor.

A Norman voice shouted, "What eez going on down 'ere?"

It was the camp commander.

And Bronwen answered, as cool as you like, "These men are making trouble and we'd like to come up again."

I almost laughed. The cheek of her! Hild and Oz were grinning, although we'd just been fighting for our lives, and when Bron walked forward, head held high, the men who'd been baying for her blood stood meekly aside and let her pass. It flashed through my mind that perhaps she *was* a witch...but no. She was just Bronwen and I hadn't begun to plumb her amazing inner depths.

"Come up, zen," said the commander, and Bron climbed the ladder, followed by Oz, Hild and me. And so we found ourselves once more in that ruined chamber with the huge orange moon staring down at us above the broken walls and rubble.

"Where did you get zese weapons?" demanded the commander.

"We found them down there," I said.

"And what were you doing down zere?" he went on.

Silence. Then Oz spoke up. "We went down for our weapons, because we'd been here before and we'd hidden them down there."

The commander shook his head.

"None of zis makes sense, but anyway, you must give zem up. Prisoners are not allowed weapons. And zen you must tell me what 'appened down zere. Why are zere so many dead bodies?"

"They attacked us," I said, "and we fought back."

The commander sighed.

"I do not understand all zis, but anyway...Guilbert! You and your men take zeir swords!"

"I don't think you'll find that very easy," said Hild.

And sure enough, as the Normans tried to relieve us of our precious weapons, the swords resisted. It was as if they were stuck to our hands.

"What do you play at?" shouted an exasperated Guilbert.

"We're not doing anything," I tried to explain. "It's the swords."

"Yeah," said Oz. "they're magic. That's why we wanted them back."

"What rubbish ees zis?" roared the commander. "Men, take zese swords from ze prisoners!"

Then followed a kind of comic dance, with the Normans trying to pull the swords out of our hands and the swords refusing to be pulled. Until it wasn't funny any more. One of the Normans tried to hack at Hild's hand, but before his weapon reached her wrist, Hild's seax twisted the attacking sword out of his grasp. It flew over the other side of the chamber and the man cursed. I guessed he felt stupid being beaten by a girl much smaller than him.

"We won't hurt anyone," I said, "but you can see our swords really are magic, so you'd best let us go."

"Let you go?" shouted the commander. "Are you mad? Men, surround zem!"

"Excuse me," said Bronwen, and ducked underneath the arm of the Norman who'd been trying to disarm her.

Nimble as a cat climbing a wall, she scrambled up the side of the chamber until she reached a broken piece where she could stand. As a soldier tried to climb after her she threw back her head and yelled with all her might.

"Tanllyd! Tanllyd!"

The Normans had loosened their grip on the rest of us while Bron was climbing, and now she turned to us and said, "Outside, quick!"

We shoved our captors out of the way, and dashed back into the main hall and then out through the ruined walls, while around us all was chaos. Everyone was awake and English and Normans mingled together with a few Welshmen, trying to see what was happening. Bron had scrambled down the other side of the chamber wall and she soon joined us.

"What are you doing? What's going on?" I muttered, grabbing her arm.

"We've got to get somewhere higher up," she panted.

"Zere she is, get 'er!" yelled a Norman voice, but it was interrupted by a scream.

"Look! A devil's coming!" shrieked an English voice. "Save yourselves!"

CHAPTER FORTY

Someone was pointing upwards and then *everyone* was looking up. Westward, in the distance was a little point of light, a fiery arrow winging its way towards us. We four took advantage of being ignored and clambered up a low broken wall. Then we stood fascinated, like everyone else, as the fiery being flew at incredible speed, growing as it approached. Suddenly people were fleeing or diving under things in a vain effort to keep themselves safe.

But Oz and I knew what it was, what Bronwen had been calling. Oz put his arm round Hild, who hadn't a clue, and I heard him tell her it was all right, we'd be rescued now.

And then, circling to find a landing place, enormous – and terrifying, even though we knew her, bronze scales gleaming in the light of the orange moon, flames shooting from her fanged mouth, came the dragon.

"Oh, Tanllyd!" called Bron ecstatically, followed by a stream of Welsh.

I didn't know any Welsh – it sounded beautiful and I'd have to learn – but I knew she was thanking Tanllyd, and I really wanted to join in.

"But how did she get here so quickly?" asked Oz, echoing my own thoughts.

"She'd told me," said Bron. "She said, wherever we were, if we needed her, just call. I think she can fly really, really fast if she wants."

"You're telling me!" said Oz.

Hild, who'd been gaping at the circling dragon, now gaped at Bron. Meanwhile, Tanllyd obviously decided there wasn't anywhere better to land than the central courtyard so she flapped her enormous batlike wings a few times, stretched out all four clawed feet and touched the ground. Then she settled down, pulling in her wings like a bird roosting.

Everywhere was deserted as Normans and English alike had fled from the dragon, and relief swept through me. No more fighting.

Bron leapt down from our broken wall and ran to Tanllyd. Then she swept a deep curtsey. We joined her, and me and Oz bowed low, while Hild copied Bron's curtsey. She was quick off the mark, that girl, and not easily scared.

And then the dragon spoke. I saw Hild jump back a little, though Oz and I managed to stay still. That voice! I'd forgotten how strange it was, how unlike any human voice. It was deep and creaky and harsh and grating, like no other sound I'd heard. Except…I remembered the first time I'd heard the dragon speak. It had reminded me of two swords scraping against each other. A dangerous sound.

But it was interrupted.

Suddenly a shower of arrows sped through the air and bounced uselessly off Tanllyd's scales. And then her voice changed! A hideous roar erupted from the dragon's throat as she lifted her head. And then a terrifying burst of flames, aimed in the direction the arrows had come from. And then screams!...And then silence.

"Quick!" said Bronwen. "Oz and Hild between those spikes at the front and Wulf and me between these two."

It wasn't easy climbing up the dragon's hot, scaly side to get to the top, though she tried to help by extending her wing a little, to give us a foothold. But we managed, driven on by panic. No more fighting I'd thought, but now every heartbeat I was expecting an arrow in my back.

We were hardly settled when both wings stretched out and flapped, causing a gale force wind so that we hung on with all our might. And then she rose in the air and we were off!

That was a wild ride. Bron had her arms tight around me as we flew higher and faster.

"Where are we going?" I shouted back, hanging on to the spike in front of me as Bron hung on to me.

"To the castle!" she shouted above the beating of the gigantic wings. "That's what she was saying when we were so rudely interrupted!"

I suppose this must have been a leisurely flight to Tanllyd, nowhere near as rapid as her lightning bolt journey to save us, but it felt like riding the wind. The ground below us flashed by so fast that I could hardly distinguish field from forest, river from road, even though the moon shone almost as brightly as the early morning sun. And then…there *was* the early morning sun. The sky behind us lightened as we sped on westwards and the pearly glow gradually spread over the whole of the heavens.

I looked overhead, still hanging on tight though my arms were aching, and I felt that beautiful morning light fill my whole being. We were free. We'd done what Woden wanted and now we had our lives back. The Normans were still here, it was true, but at that moment it didn't seem so important. I had Bronwen and we could be together.

And there in the distance were the mountains of Wales and Gethin's castle. But we didn't have to go into that dark fortress and face unknown monsters. We could just walk away. After we'd thanked Tanllyd, of course.

One good thing about riding on a dragon is that the fire in its belly stops you freezing to death, however high you fly. So when she circled round and delicately put her great clawed feet on the ground, we were not blocks of ice. But we were still pretty stiff and uncomfortable as we slid down her scaly sides on to the ground. She'd landed by that break in the hills that led into the valley where stood Gethin's castle. We shook our achy limbs and did lots of bowing and curtseying while Bron had a long conversation with our rescuer.

Then Tanllyd reared her head and gazed at us all, her golden cat's eyes with their vertical black slits showing no emotion that we could read. She might as well have been wondering whether she fancied us for breakfast for all I could tell. But she'd saved us and we trusted her, and most of all we trusted Bron. Then the dragon dipped her head, we did one more bow and curtsey, and she turned into the valley, her long body and even longer tail snaking through that little break in the ring of hills. We watched her go in silence.

Of course it was Oz who broke the stillness.

"So what do we do now?" he said.

CHAPTER FORTY-ONE

Suddenly I felt my legs would hardly hold me up.

"I'm exhausted," I said.

"I'm starving," said Oz.

"I'm both of those things," said Hild.

Bronwen laughed. "Why don't we go back to my hut, it's not far from here. We might be able to rustle up something to eat, I'm not sure, but at least we can sleep in safety."

So we trudged back to Bronwen's little hut in the forest, over the moorland where we'd seen the hare and Bron had stopped us shooting it with our bows and arrows. We didn't have bows now, so hunting wouldn't be easy, but I knew things would work out all right. I smiled as I remembered the delight I'd felt at seeing Bronwen again, how unbelievable it had seemed.

And there was the hermit's hut and there, like a miracle, was a basket of food. Bron clapped her hands.

"Do you remember I told you I still had some friends in the village not far from here? And they bring me food sometimes? Well, today is our lucky day."

"In more ways than one," said Hild.

There were turnips, apples, onions and a cabbage. But more importantly for us now, there were two small fowl, plucked and cooked, probably partridge by the size, a large cheese and a fresh loaf! The fowl would have made two good meals for Bron, though only half a meal each for the four of us. But with the bread, cheese and apples, the whole thing seemed like a feast and we flung ourselves on the ground and set to.

After a while we could talk as well as eat and we spoke vaguely about making our way to the village of Hild's aunt, where her mother had gone.

Bron said that first she should go and say goodbye and thank you to her village friends. Then Oz said something that had been on my mind. Something I'd been worrying about.

"You know," he said, "I'm not sure what we *are* going to do now, but I've got a horrible feeling we ought to rejoin the resistance."

And then I knew the solution to my problem.

"No point," I shrugged, "after what Woden told us."

"What *did* Woden tell you?" asked Hild eagerly. I knew she was in awe of what *she* felt was my connection with the god, but what *I* felt was him picking on me, asking me to do nearly impossible things.

"That we've already lost," I said, and watched as her face fell in disbelief.

"But he's a god of war, as well as of the runes," she protested. "Surely he wouldn't want you to give up."

"What *exactly* did he say?" demanded Oz. "Can you remember his exact words?"

"Actually, I can," I said, "because I was so stunned."

Then I found myself back in that clearing in the fir trees where I had first met him. I could smell the pine and hear the crackle of the fire. Suddenly I felt a stirring in me as if adventures shouldn't yet be over.

Woden smiled. As ever, he knew what I was thinking. I asked about rejoining our forces, fighting the Normans, and he said, 'Forget that! That war is lost!'

I remember, I felt as if my head would burst. The one thing that had kept us going was the thought that…we could get rid of the invader. And now Woden was telling us to give up.

'You're supposed to be the god of battle!' I shouted. 'How can you tell us to give up?'

Woden bowed his head and stood silent for a few moments. Then he sighed and went on in his deep voice, 'It is not easy for me to say that. England has been defeated but she will rise again…gradually. And one day she will be truly great.'

And those were his exact words. He pierced me with his one dark eye and I found myself gradually back with my friends. The feeling of lightness returned.

Everyone looked at me and no-one said a thing. Then Oz spoke.

"You know what," he said. "We're too tired to think now, let alone make decisions. Let's go to sleep."

And we did just that, on the ground outside Bron's hut, without even setting a guard. Stupid, I know, but who would have been able to keep themselves awake? Besides, I think we all felt as if we were in a bubble of good luck, ever since Tanllyd had turned up. And we were deeply, desperately tired.

When I came to, the sun was waning and Bron had started to gather a few things together from her hut, things that we might need on our travels. There was an autumn smell in the air and an evening chill. We picked at what was left of our meal and watched through the branches of the trees as the moon rose. Not the huge orange moon of last night but a beautiful silvery globe. I still felt that everything around us was enchanted and that all our choices would be good ones. I also felt it was up to me to say something.

"What we were talking about," I started, "about what Woden said. I honestly think he'd want us to stay alive, and not waste our lives on a lost cause."

No-one replied. Eventually Hild said, "So what will we do then?"

"Well, Oz and I both know how to farm, to grow things, and I'm sure your brother could let us have a few sheep."

Hild made a face. "Sheep don't like me," she said.

Then Oz joined in. "Bron can work her magic on them and make them do what you say, and you can do the practical stuff."

Bron smiled. Hild didn't.

"Don't worry, Hild," I said, we'll find something we all enjoy doing."

Hild put her arms round her knees and smiled at me. "You're so understanding, Wulf," she said.

Oz shrugged.

"We're all good with a bow and arrow," I said.

"Which we haven't got," said Oz.

"But we could make some," put in Bron.

"We need yew trees, they're the best, they don't break," objected Oz.

"Surely some other trees would do for now?" said Bron.

"And you can help me find them," said Oz to Hild, who was brightening by now.

Hild grinned at him. We got up from the ground and brushed ourselves down.

"And when we get to this village of Hild's aunt," said Bron, "there might be a puppy we can have."

At this, Hild brightened considerably more. Bron really knew the right thing to say.

"Yeah," I said. "In the spring we'll go a bit further in and find a good place for a smallholding. But for now let's get to the village. I mean it'd be different," I went on, "if we had any chance of success, but Woden *told* us it was a lost cause." I began to feel more confident. "So it seems to me that we have to live our lives the best way we can, facing danger if it comes our way, but not searching for it. You know, looking out for each other and just being, well, the best we can be."

Suddenly Oz grinned.

"And thus ends the sermon of Father Wulfstan."

I grinned back, and then I flung myself on him and we rolled over and over as if we were little kids again, while the girls sat and laughed.

So when we set off together there was a lightness in our step, despite the dangers around us, despite knowing that the Normans were in our beloved land. Somehow, in the end things would turn out all right. I held Bron's hand. Inside my shirt I could feel the little bag with her amber necklace in. The necklace I was going to put around her neck on the day we got married.

ACKNOWLEDGEMENTS

Jo and Tony thank her writing workshop for their endless support, inspiration and friendship: Penny Joelson, Angela Kanter, Vivien Boyes and Derek Rhodes. Special thanks to Angela for proof reading and editing, and both Penny and Angela for all their help with publishing. Thanks to Reena Patel for her imagination and talent, and her third amazing cover art work, and to Helen Hart and all at SilverWood Books for their helpfulness and consistently high quality design.

ALSO BY JO BARNES

Odd Fox Out

Have you ever had a chance meeting which changed your life?
That's what happens to Edgar Sharpeyes when he is a small fox cub...

ISBN 978-1-80042-247-6

Available in paperback and as an ebook

www.ingramcontent.com/pod-product-compliance
Lightning Source LLC
La Vergne TN
LVHW090940080826
845145LV00003B/833

* 9 7 8 1 8 0 0 4 2 3 1 3 8 *